'It looks bad, but Ben's one of the truly strong ones. If anyone can pull through this he can. With *your* help.' The nurse smiled encouragingly. 'Your husband's a hero.'

Your husband's a hero?

Nausea churned Thea's stomach. Her mouth was parched—too parched to respond. It took her several attempts to swallow, then flick out a nervous tongue to try to moisten dry lips.

Her husband?

For the first time since she'd heard about the accident and rushed in to the hospital Thea felt her pain and fear give way to something even more visceral.

Anger.

The man lying in that bed—her husband—was almost as much of a stranger to her as he was to the nurse standing next to her now. That was if Thea set aside the fact that the last time she'd seen Ben they'd had wild, crazy sex, only for him to walk out on her the next morning. Leaving her abandoned and alone. It was a far cry from the Ben everyone else saw—the self-sacrificing soldier who had always seemed to save the day in her brother's war stories. Where had Ben the hero been when *she'd* needed saving?

Instead, she'd had to save herself.

So why, even now, did he still have the power to affect her the way he did?

Dear Reader,

Thank you for picking *The Army Doc's Secret Wife*—
my debut novel for Mills & Boon Medical Romance.
I'm so proud and honoured to be a writer within
the M&B family. I picked up my first M&B at
fifteen—when a school friend lent me one from her
collection—and I was hooked.

I love high-octane heroes, and I'm so proud of our
soldiers—who are prepared to lay down their lives
to protect their country, whether they agree with the
politicians or not.

My very own hero is my former Troop Commander—
a shy young man who nonetheless was a stickler for
discipline. We resisted the sparks of attraction for
three years whilst I was an Officer Cadet under his
command… But I wondered what would happen if
my hero and heroine, Ben and Thea, were caught up
in a more emotional situation, with Ben's terrible
survivor's guilt over the death of Thea's brother
playing a part in the way he responds to her.

The idea of a second chance at love also appealed—
especially as my hero walked away for such
honourable reasons. But Thea is no pushover. She's a
high-flying professional in more than one sense of the
term and, having been hurt in the past, has an inner
core of steel. As much as she loves her hero, she's
determined to help Ben beat his demons before she
opens herself up to him again.

I hope you enjoy *The Army Doc's Secret Wife*,
and I'd love it if you dropped by my website—
charlottehawkes.com.

Charlotte

THE ARMY DOC'S
SECRET WIFE

BY
CHARLOTTE HAWKES

Published in Great Britain 2016
By Mills & Boon, an imprint of HarperCollins*Publishers*
1 London Bridge Street, London, SE1 9GF

© 2016 Charlotte Hawkes

ISBN: 978-0-263-06476-6

Our policy is to use papers that are natural, renewable and recyclable
products and made from wood grown in sustainable forests. The logging
and manufacturing processes conform to the legal environmental
regulations of the country of origin.

Printed and bound in Great Britain
by CPI Antony Rowe, Chippenham, Wiltshire

Born and raised on the Wirral Peninsula, England, **Charlotte Hawkes** is mum to two intrepid boys who love her to play building block games with them and who object loudly to the amount of time she spends on the computer. When she isn't writing—or building with blocks—she is company director for a small Anglo/French construction company. Charlotte loves to hear from readers, and you can contact her at her website: charlottehawkes.com.

The Army Doc's Secret Wife
is **Charlotte Hawkes**'s debut title
for Mills & Boon Medical Romance!

To my beautiful boys, Montgomery and Bartholomew.
You may never read these books, but—for the record—
one of you is very excited that you're almost able to
read the back of your pirate bubblebath bottle!

To my parents,
for your unfailing love and support throughout my life—
even if you *do* now spoil my boys terribly.

To Flo, my editor, for getting me here.
You whipped me—and my book—into incredible shape.
Don't stop *hmmmmm*-ing!

To my husband, my real-life hero (& Capt.).
Without you, none of this would be possible.
Sorry(ish) about the *Sir* stuff.

CHAPTER ONE

ICY NUMBNESS HAD been sneaking around Alethea 'Thea' Abrams' body from the moment she'd received the phone call. The drive to the hospital was a blur but somehow she must have done it. And now the chill finally took a grip of her shaking limbs, forcing her to stop and lean on the door frame as if to draw strength, as she stared down the military wing's ward and into the side room where Ben Abrams, her husband, lay—still asleep—in a bed.

'I understand you've been fully briefed?' The nurse consulted her notes. 'And that you're also a civilian doctor, working for the Air Ambulance Emergency Response Unit? That'll certainly help a lot. And Dr Fields *has* prepared you for the chance that Major Abrams... Ben...might not recognise you?'

Thea managed a stiff nod, surreptitiously sliding cold fingers around the doorjamb. *Yes, they had warned her it was a possibility.* Words of caution she often had to say to other people, and yet it had still been a shock to hear them said to her. It all felt surreal—like some kind of nightmare. The broken body in that bed was so far removed from the robust, spirited, dynamic Ben she knew.

If she had ever really known him.

'I understand how difficult this is but you need to be ready. Your reaction could influence how Ben approaches his recovery.' The nurse was kind but firm.

'I understand.' Miraculously, Thea made it sound as if she did, despite the fact that the professional, medical side of her brain appeared to have completely deserted her.

'Are you ready to go over there?'

Thea watched as Dr Fields moved around Ben's bed. There was another man there, an older man who looked vaguely familiar, but Thea couldn't place him. He wasn't interfering, and she couldn't tell whether he was overseeing or not. An Army specialist perhaps? Not anyone she knew.

Not trusting herself to speak, Thea forced out a couple more jerky nods. The nurse seemed unconvinced.

'Listen, it's a lot to take in all at once. Do you need a few more moments? We can go to the visitors' room—it's just down the corridor.'

Thea shook her head, unable to drag her gaze from Ben, who looked so utterly alien to her, and yet so painfully familiar at the same time.

'Just run me through it again.' Her voice was so hoarse she couldn't even recognise it herself. 'Ben was caught in a roadside bomb?'

'Yes—well, two, actually. His vehicle was the fourth in a convoy, and the IED was detonated as the second four-by-four passed. Ben was quite severely injured in the initial blast, severing his arm at the level of the proximal humerus, and he has since undergone successful micro-vascular replantation. However, even with that level of injury we understand he ran to the front vehicles to pull out the rest of his patrol.'

The utter admiration in the military nurse's voice was evident, but Thea just stared at the uncharacteristically still figure in the bed, a maelstrom swirling in her head.

Dammit, Ben—you nearly died. Why do you always have to play the hero?

How was she meant to correlate this with the life-loving Ben who had always lived for his beloved sports?

'He pulled five soldiers to safety—he saved their lives—before the second IED went off, and then he was crushed under a vehicle and knocked unconscious.'

'Which is when he sustained the spinal damage,' Thea

stated flatly, her medical brain finally—mercifully—
kicking in. She needed to detach herself from her unsteady
emotions. It was the only way she was going to get through
this. *If only it was that easy,* she thought bleakly.

'It looks bad, but from what we've seen, Ben is strong.
If anyone can pull through this, he can. With your help.'
The nurse smiled encouragingly. 'Your husband's a hero.'

Your husband's a hero.

Nausea churned in Thea's stomach. Her mouth was
parched—too parched to respond. It took her several attempts to swallow, then to flick out a nervous tongue to
try and moisten dry lips.

Her husband...

For the first time since she'd heard about the accident
and rushed to the hospital Thea felt her pain and fear give
way to something even more visceral.

Anger.

The man lying in that bed—her husband—was almost
as much of a stranger to her as he was to the nurse standing
next to her now. That was if Thea set aside the fact that the
last time she'd seen Ben they'd had wild, crazy sex, only
for him to walk out on her the next morning. Leaving her
abandoned and alone. That was a far cry from the Ben everyone else saw—the self-sacrificing soldier who always
seemed to save the day in her brother's war stories. Where
had Ben the hero been when *she'd* needed saving?

Instead, she'd had to save herself.

So why, even now, did he still have the power to affect
her the way he did?

'I understand your husband has been hailed as a hero
before?' The nurse broke into Thea's preoccupation with
another encouraging smile. 'Wasn't he awarded the Distinguished Service Order?'

'He was part of a patrol that was ambushed.' Thea forced
herself to acknowledge the question, her tongue feeling too

thick for her mouth. 'Ben took out at least twenty of the enemy before back-up arrived.'

'I can believe it.' The nurse smiled, shaking her head incredulously. 'And his patrol mates?'

'That's all I know.' Thea heaved her shoulders and fought back tears. She didn't want to talk any more—didn't want to tell the nurse that Ben's patrol mate—her own brother Daniel—had died. Having already lost her parents when she was nine years old, Daniel had been all she'd had, and back then the pain of losing him had been raw. She hadn't asked Ben exactly what had happened, and he had never spoken about it.

'Can you just give me a few moments, please?' Thea asked the nurse, grateful when she nodded her understanding and moved away to give Thea some space.

This was harder than she could have imagined. This one event had opened a floodgate of emotions and memories she'd kept locked away for almost two decades.

After their parents' death it had been just her and Daniel, but whilst she'd stayed with foster families—twice being offered and turning down a permanent home—her brother, seven years older than her, had remained in the children's home. No one had wanted a teenage boy. Hardly surprising that Daniel had joined the Army the day he'd turned eighteen.

The day Thea had turned eighteen she'd thanked her kindly foster family, packed her bag, and left to be reunited with her brother. Looking back, she realised that moving from the free accommodation within the Army barracks to renting a tiny flat in town for them both must have taken every penny Daniel had—and yet he'd never once made her feel anything other than welcome.

Three years later he'd been killed in that ambush and she'd gone to pieces, fallen in with the wrong crowd. It seemed doubly ironic that Ben—the one person who had tracked her down night after night and dragged her out of illegal warehouse raves, the one person who had stayed with her until the very worst of the grief had started to clear and she'd been able to see that being hell-bent on self-destruction wasn't the way to go—should have walked out on her too, leaving her more alone than ever.

Of all the losses in her life, none had left her feeling as abandoned, as *bereft*, as when Ben had walked out on her. Except perhaps the loss of their baby. *Ben's* baby. Thea pushed away a surge of nausea but couldn't tear her mind away from the devastating memory.

When Ben, barely twenty-five years old, had offered her marriage Thea, just twenty-one herself, and looking for someone to cling to after Daniel's death, had jumped at it. With hindsight, Ben's subsequent walking out on her had been inevitable.

Daniel had once claimed that Ben had always appeared older than his years. Something to do with a regimented upbringing and a strict Army Colonel father, which had left Ben with an overdeveloped sense of responsibility for everything and everyone around him.

And Ben had honoured the *responsibility* side of their marriage. His Captain's income had given her security, money to fund her continued education and a home of her own—not that he'd ever returned to it after their wedding night. If he hadn't done all that, where would she have ended up? Certainly not as one of the youngest doctors with the Air Ambulance, that was for sure.

She would have to keep reminding herself that *that* was why she was here. Not because she still cared about Ben, but because she owed him a great debt. However much he had hurt her.

Nothing could ever completely erase the pain of losing the people who had loved her the most, but the one consolation she'd always held on to was the fact that both her parents and her brother had been ripped from her against their will—they hadn't abandoned her.

But Ben was different. He had *chosen* to leave her. Worse still, he had walked out on her the morning after their wedding. The morning after their wedding *night*— when she had thought they had made the ultimate connection.

She'd been wrong.

'Dr Abrams?' Thea hadn't noticed the nurse return, and she swung around to meet her gentle gaze.

'I'll be over at the nurses' station—just let me know when you'd like to go in to see your husband.'

'Great,' Thea croaked.

What the hell was she supposed to say to him?

Her mind whirled. This was a walk of shame and an oh-so-awkward morning-after conversation all rolled into one. And to make matters worse it was five years too late.

She squeezed her eyes shut, as if blocking the memories which suddenly threatened to engulf her. *She had to stop being silly.* No doubt the last time they'd been together— the awkward sex—was the least of Ben's problems right now. Besides, nothing good could come of wallowing. She knew that from bitter experience. It might have taken her almost all of these five years to come to terms with what had happened, but she had finally managed to.

At least she'd thought she had. The moment she'd received that call—shocked that she was still noted as Ben's next of kin—and seen him lying immobile in that bed, her emotions had been whipped into a confused mess.

Ben was hurt. She couldn't ever forgive him for abandoning her emotionally when she'd needed him, but she had to concede that he hadn't abandoned his responsibility to her. Now he needed *her* help, and she couldn't ignore the sense of commitment that struck in her—half buried as it might be. She owed him loyalty for that, at least.

She stuffed the anger back down, feeling calmer as the genuine concern she felt for him slowly started to regain control over her errant emotions. Perhaps seeing Ben through this, helping him to recover, would be the closure she finally needed? She had no choice. It was proving impossible to put Major Ben Abrams into her past any other way.

Thea felt a tiny sliver of resolve harden in her chest—her strong, professional inner core finally peeking its head out again—and she clutched at it before it darted back into the shadows. Tilting up her head, she urged her leaden legs to move in the direction of the nurses' station just as the nurse glanced up.

'Dr Abrams? Are you ready to go in now?'

Thea jutted out her chin and fell back on all her training. It offered her a much needed confidence boost.

'So...' Thea injected as much authority into her tone as possible. 'What's the prognosis?'

It barely took a moment for the nurse to register the difference in her. She shot Thea a look more akin to one colleague looking at another, rather than at a patient's next of kin.

'Fortunately the ambush occurred not far from the camp, and they were able to get a team out quickly to secure the area and recover the casualties. Ben was med-evacced to the nearest main hospital, which was when his arm was reattached. The seven-hour operation went smoothly, but there will be follow-ups, of course.'

'And what about regaining normal function?' Thea asked. That sliver of resolve was starting to grow, lending Thea a new sense of determination.

'Under ideal circumstances, with consistent physio and positive rehabilitation, Major Abrams can expect to regain up to eighty-five per cent of normal function.'

Eighty-five per cent of normal function? Ben was a surgeon.

Thea suppressed a shudder. How would he cope with never being able to operate again? What was more, these weren't *ideal* circumstances.

She could see the concern in the nurse's eyes.

'I'm guessing that with Ben's additional spinal injury that replantation prognosis is optimistic? What level of spinal injury is it?'

'Honestly…? We simply don't know at this stage.' The nurse shook her head. 'We know the bomb blast was significant, and that Major Abrams went into spinal shock. So there is spinal cord damage. But the swelling means we have no idea just how extensive the damage is.'

Thea nodded grimly, struggling to keep those icy fingers from curling their way around her heart again.

'I appreciate you're Air Ambulance,' the nurse was saying, 'but how much do you know about spinal injuries post-emergency rescue?'

'These days it's mainly assessing, securing and stabilising the patient to ensure no further damage during transport,' Thea acknowledged. 'As you say, I don't usually get involved with the post-emergency rescue care. But before I joined the Air Ambulance I did do some work on the Keimen case.'

It was one of the things which had helped to propel her up the career ladder at such a young age. That and her driving need to block out the pain caused by Ben's ultimate rejection.

'The boy whose spinal cord was completely severed and who took his first steps some two years later?'

Thea dipped her head. The work had been cutting edge, and she wasn't surprised that it had caught the nurse's attention.

'I understand they transplanted cells from the part of the brain involved in sending smell signals from the nose to the brain to stimulate the repair of his spinal cord?'

'That's right.' Thea managed a smile despite herself. It had been inspiring to work on that case.

'I see.' The nurse nodded. 'Then you'll completely understand the difficulty at the moment with Major Abrams.

As I said, there's still too much swelling to get a clear MRI, and unfortunately we do know that the impact of the second IED and the Land Rover crushing him was significant.'

'So it's a waiting game,' Thea stated as calmly as she could.

As unlikely as it sounded, she could only hope that the swelling was protecting his back and that any injury was as low down as possible. Usually, the lower it was, the better. The sacral nerves, perhaps, at worst the lumbar. But the higher the damage—the thoracic nerves or, God forbid, somewhere within the cervical vertebrae—the more chance Ben might be paralysed for life.

Thea squeezed her eyes shut at the thought. Ben was such a physical guy—not just as a soldier but in his personal life, too. She couldn't imagine how he would react to such news, but she would need to start considering options just in case. He loved sports. *All* sports. Mountain biking, climbing, kayaking—even base jumping. And their fake honeymoon had been a skiing trip—not that they'd gone after he'd walked out.

Before that failed night Ben had promised to take her, after she'd told him that the highlight of her years in and out of care homes had been a charity group who'd taken a bunch of them to some rundown hostel every year.

Thea shook her head before the memory could get a grip. It was those caring, thoughtful moments from Ben which had meant that the same morning he'd walked out—the morning after they'd made love for the first time—Thea had been screwing up all her courage to suggest that one day they might possibly have more than just a fake marriage. Even if it took time.

Odd, the randomness of the memories which now popped into her head...

'Yes, it's a waiting game,' the nurse confirmed sympathetically.

Thea blinked slowly. *Ben didn't know any of this yet.* She

stood for a moment, looking down the ward in silence. Life was precious,—so very precious. Why was it that people lost sight of that so easily—including her? *Especially* her.

Abruptly she stepped forward, as if to steel her body as well as her mind, and headed to the side room. As she got closer she could see the traction which stopped Ben from moving his neck and back, his legs, until they were able to assess the damage. He looked so uncharacteristically fragile that she felt her emotions start to bubble once again.

Ben—who had rejected her not once, but twice, leaving her broken. And yet it seemed entirely fitting that, as she stood by his bedside, across from the nurse as she checked his vitals, Ben chose that moment to wake up.

'Thea? What are you doing here?'

He recognised her!

She blinked back tears as the nurse swung around to pour a beaker of fresh water and offer a straw for Ben to take a sip. He was clearly still groggy from the sedatives, and his brain was no doubt a mush of memories that he wouldn't be able to process or even arrange in chronological order. But the fact that he knew who she was an encouraging start. And, despite the painful rasp, the unexpected warmth in his voice at seeing her had caught her off guard. But it had also made her feel more helpless than she'd ever felt before. It was as if the last five years had momentarily been erased.

She wouldn't cry, she *wouldn't*.

'I'm sorry. I'm so sorry...' His voice cracked as he struggled to speak. 'About Daniel...about the wedding...'

'Shh...don't talk. Just rest.' She blinked furiously to stop the unwelcome tears from falling. Tears of fear, but also of relief.

So much for the concern that he might not remember anything. She should have known better—this was Ben Abrams they were dealing with. She should have known he would fight through.

'I'm sorry about everything...'

His slurred words were barely clear, but she could de-cipher them.

'I'll protect you, Thea. I'll never leave you again.'

It was absurd that her heart should lurch so unexpect-edly. Thea chastised herself. It was the medication talk-ing—she knew that—and even groggy he wasn't saying the three words she had once longed to hear. Though no longer. There weren't *any* words she wanted to hear from him any more.

Caught up in her thoughts, Thea realised too late that Ben was fighting to move his arm and take her hand. His injured arm. As if in slow motion she watched him strug-gle to raise his head, only for the restraints to stop him. His eyes slid to the damaged limb as it lay obstinately on the bed, refusing to obey the commands his brain was sending out.

This was happening all wrong. She needed to speak to him, explain things to him—not have him find out for himself...especially not like this. In horror, she saw Ben stare at the arm, then down to the other restraints around his pelvis and spine. Finally came the realisation of mem-ory, and it chased long, furious shadows across his bruised face. His eyes met hers one final time.

'Get her out of here. *Now*,' he snarled, his eyes unex-pectedly full of accusation and despair and loathing before he abruptly passed out again.

Did he still blame her for that night? That night when she'd barely been able to think straight with grief. That night she'd craved just a few moments of dark oblivion, to forget everything. An oblivion that only crazy, stupid sex with Ben might have momentarily brought.

Emotions rushed to crowd in on her, dense and suffocat-ing. Her initial relief had been swallowed up in pain, anger, frustration, sympathy and misplaced love. They coursed around her body, leaving her weak and nauseous.

Pain gripped her heart. This wasn't about *her*—she knew that—and yet she couldn't help reliving her utter devastation of almost five years earlier. It wasn't right that this should be the first time she'd seen him since he'd walked out. It wasn't right that he should be lying there so battered and broken. And it wasn't right that—even like this—he still had the power to hurt her.

A strangled sob escaped her throat before she could stop it. Her emotions were pushed to the limit. And suddenly all she could think about was the baby she had conceived as a result of that one incredible night. *Their* baby—although he'd never known. Almost five years on, she could still feel the pain which had torn at her heart the day she'd lost it.

Another sob threatened to break free and she choked it back just as Dr Fields came back into the room.

'It's just the sedative talking.' He looked up at her sharply before softening his voice. 'Think of Ben like any other patient, if it helps. Don't let it get to you, Doctor.'

She bowed her head, unable to speak and yet unable to leave the room.

The surgeon continued. 'His vitals are stable. Rest is the best thing to help his body to heal at this time, and I've no doubt that, despite his initial reaction, seeing you will help to calm any fears he has and help him to be patient until we know more.'

Thea wasn't so sure. But when Ben woke up she'd finally have to tell him. *Everything.* Yes, she definitely needed closure.

CHAPTER TWO

Five years earlier

'SHOULD I…? THAT IS…do you want me to carry you over the threshold?' Ben hesitated at the cottage door, his key still unturned in the lock.

'Sorry?'

Her voice sounded thick, as if she was in some kind of fug. He could empathise with that.

'Now we're married…' Ben shrugged, feeling uncharacteristically helpless. He didn't *do* emotion at the best of times. But Thea's brother—his best friend—had just died. How was he supposed to support her? 'I just wondered…'

He trailed off, hating these alien feelings. His career depended on him being decisive and sure. He gathered the best intelligence he could and made his plan of action accordingly. But how did he gather intel on the right way to help a grieving sister? How did he ensure he said the right thing, *did* the right thing? He didn't know the right protocols. He didn't know the rules. It left him feeling ineffective and uncertain.

But he *did* know it was now his responsibility to help Thea. And that ignoring loss, pretending it didn't exist, didn't make it go away. He knew *that* from bitter experience.

'I don't know if I'm expected to carry you over the threshold,' he stated uncomfortably.

'Oh. No, *Lord, no*—of course not.' Thea shook her head

in distress. 'I just want to get into the house and off this street. I can practically *feel* the curtains twitching.'

Ben glanced around. Not a single curtain had moved, but he could understand Thea's discomfort and her need to escape inside.

Marrying someone with whom he'd only been on one date wasn't something he'd ever thought he would do. He wasn't impulsive. At least not in his personal life. But this wasn't about impulsiveness. It was about practicality. It was about fulfilling his promise to Dan—Thea's brother and his army buddy—that he would take care of Thea. The guy had taken a bullet for him—fulfilling that promise was a given.

Ben had taken over payment of the fees for Thea's medical degree, given her access to other necessary finances, but finding her a new home had been harder, given the time constraints. Her landlord had evicted her the moment he'd discovered Dan was dead and she could no longer pay the rent. Finding her a new flat would have taken more time than he had.

The only solution had been to marry her, so that the Army would allocate them a house within the officers' married quarters on the base. With its tight-knit community, and the fact that he was often away on courses, exercises and tours of duty, he'd thought it the safest place for a twenty-one-year-old girl who had already lost her parents at...what had Dan said...eight? Nine?

'I'm just not used to all...*this*.' Thea waved her hand in the direction of the cul-de-sac as Ben opened the door and she practically fell inside.

'Community?'

She shook her head. 'People knowing your business.'

There were boxes in the hallway. He hadn't had time to sort anything out yet, although neither of them owned much stuff. She didn't seem to hang on to personal effects; that was something they both had in common.

'It's...pretty,' she sounded surprised. 'Until the other

day, I'd always assumed married quarters just meant a different wing in the barracks,'

'No. Married soldiers get a house either on, or near to, the camp,'Ben dredged up a smile. 'The higher rank the soldier is, the nicer the accommodation. And the quieter the area on camp.'

'Right,' Thea nodded robotically.

He doubted if she had even really seen the place properly when the Housing Officer had marched them in a week ago to take inventory and do a damage report. She had still been coming to terms with burying Dan.

He knew Dan hadn't been able to afford to rent more than a one-bedroom flat for his sister, so she could have a roof over her head. He had always put Thea first.

Dan had been a great medic, but he would have made a great doctor—a great officer. Just as Ben was. The only reason Dan hadn't become one was because he hadn't been able to afford the time out for courses. The guy had signed on into the Army the moment he'd been able to, just to get out of that children's home and earn enough money to send the gifted Thea to uni when she came out of foster care.

He'd given his sister every advantage he hadn't had, and the fact that she was in the third year of her medical degree was as much down to his love and encouragement as Thea's ability.

Now Dan was gone, and Ben had promised to take on the mantle of responsibility. To put Thea first. He'd be damned if he was going to betray the promise he'd made to his dying buddy. But that meant he was also going to have to remember his own promise to himself never to go near the only woman he'd ever felt strongly about.

For one dangerous moment memories of their one incredible date together assailed him. Instantly Ben slammed the shutters on his mind before those memories could take hold and complicate matters. He could *not* afford to go there. He would have to keep reminding himself that he wasn't the right man for Thea. He would only end up hurting her, and she had enough to contend with.

'I thought you might feel more secure here.' Ben forced himself to go on. 'The neighbours are all army spouses too. You'll have a support network when I ship out in a few days—they'll look after you.'

'Yes, it should help,' she agreed flatly.

'Plus, getting something through the Army was the fastest thing I could do in the time frame.'

He saw her wince, regretted his directness. But the truth was he had only been given one month of compassionate leave. One month in which to break news to Thea which would destroy her whole life as she knew it. One month in which to fulfil his promise to look after Thea for life. One month to convince her that marrying him wasn't lunacy, but necessary to ensure her financial security.

'Can I get you anything? A drink? Something to eat?'

She shook her head, refusing to meet his eye. Spying her canvas clothes bag, she made a relieved grab for it. 'If you don't mind, I just want to go to bed.'

'It's barely eight-thirty,' he noted with surprise.

'It's been a long day.' Thea shrugged. 'I figure I could try to sleep. Just hope that, if I do, when I wake up it won't be this day any longer.'

'Right.' He nodded quickly. He doubted she'd slept much in the three weeks since he'd told her that Dan was dead. 'Of course. I understand.'

She was still standing there, as if waiting for him. Was he supposed to go with her? That wasn't the agreement they'd made.

'Um…which room is mine?'

She flushed a deep red and Ben cursed his lack of sensitivity. The sooner he was redeployed, the better.

'Oh, the second on the right. But we can swap later, if you prefer. I won't be here much.'

She gave an uninterested nod and, dismissing his words,

turned swiftly to head up the stairs. He heard her moving around up there as he tried to still his mind with the banal task of unpacking some of the boxes. The kettle, some mugs, teabags for a start.

He opened the first box and came face to face with a photo of himself and Dan on their first tour of duty together. This was harder than he had feared. Slamming the box shut, he grabbed a sleeping bag and followed Thea's lead, heading upstairs to the other bedroom.

Ben lay rigid and motionless on his back in the bed, his hands locked behind his head. There was no way he could sleep. He watched the numbers counting up painfully slowly on the clock projecting the time onto the ceiling. Twenty-one hundred hours. It wasn't just the time. Normally he could sleep on a clothesline, and anyway he'd been to bed at more ridiculous hours in his time on tour. It was more the fact that on the other side of the wall he could hear Thea in her own bed as she shifted, coughed and sporadically sobbed.

He had no idea if he'd done the right thing by marrying her, but he knew he was honouring his promise to Dan and that was all that really mattered. Plus, even if their marriage was fake their friendship didn't have to be. Thea was grieving, and Ben knew just what she was going through.

Unable to lie there listening to her distress, he got up off the creaking bed and ducked out of his door to knock gently on Thea's. No answer, but by the sudden silence it was clear that she had heard him. She didn't respond.

He should leave. She obviously didn't want him there. But a little voice told him she needed him. He knocked again, then turned the handle, tentatively at first.

'Thea, is there anything I can do?'

Thea was sitting up, her knees pulled to her chest. Her tense features relaxed slightly as she looked up and saw him.

He crossed the room in a couple of long strides, scooping

her up and pulling her into his arms, assiduously ignoring the pretty lacy lemon negligee. One hand secured her to him, the other smoothed her hair gently, and he let her cry it out. Holding her until she finally grew still.

When she did, he shifted as though to lower her back onto the bed.

'Don't go,' she whispered. 'Please, stay with me...just for tonight....'

'It's not a good idea.'

So why was he so tempted?

Lifting herself, Thea searched his face with red-rimmed eyes. 'Then at least talk to me, Ben.'

Talking. The thing he was least good at.

'What about?' he asked, faltering.

'Anything...' She hiccupped. 'Distract me.'

'Why did Dan always call you Ethel?' he blurted out, his mind having gone suddenly blank. 'I never knew your real name was Thea until our date. When I found out you were Dan's sister.'

Way to go, idiot. Talk about the very person she doesn't *want to think about.*

But Thea smiled. A small, fond smile which tore at Ben's heart.

'When I was a kid I couldn't pronounce Alethea, so I used to tell people my name was Ethel. Dan loved it. Even when I started to be known as Thea he still called me Ethel. It was our thing. No one else could share in it.'

'Right...' Ben swallowed uncomfortably. He wished he'd never asked. Somehow it had made him feel closer to Thea. He didn't *want* to feel closer to Thea. He clenched his fists as the image that had haunted him for the last three weeks swam into his head in high definition.

Dan...cradled in his arms as he lay dying on that hard desert ground.

Their two-man patrol had walked straight into an ambush and the two of them had been alone and pinned down by the enemy, with only a rocky outcrop for protection. Ben had tried and tried to stem the bleeding but it had been just too severe. Time had started to run out for the guy he'd fought alongside twenty-four-seven, for three hundred and twenty days of their last year's tour of duty. And for multiple tours over the last seven years before that.

Grief hovered in the back of his mind but he refused to let it in. There was no place in his mind for mourning—he had to stay strong for Thea. She didn't know the half of it. And he was never going to tell her. Besides, wasn't he the king of shutting out emotions? He'd been doing it well enough for the last decade and a half.

'Did you ever wonder how we'd never met before?' Thea asked suddenly. 'I mean, you were Daniel's best friend and I was his sister.'

'Not really.' Ben paused thoughtfully. 'Dan was always careful to keep the two sides of his life separate—his personal life and you, and his Army life. I think after your parents died he didn't have the easiest time of it in the kids' home. He never really talked about his past to anyone.'

'Except you?' Thea observed. 'Because he trusted you?'

'Right,' Ben answered bleakly.

'But still...' Thea shook her head, still confused. 'If he trusted you that much, surely you'd have come with him round to the flat?'

'No, I never came round.' Ben shrugged. 'You have to understand I'm a commissioned officer. Dan wasn't. Being part of a team and in each other's company twenty-four-seven is one thing, but socialising back home isn't that easy.'

'Because the Army don't allow it?'

Thea frowned, confused. Ben didn't blame her. The Forces had their rules, their protocols, and if you were a part of it then it all made sense. It could save lives. But to an outsider trying to understand it might seem strange.

'They don't encourage it,' Ben admitted. 'We have separate messes for socialising. But the Army *do* realise that the bonds formed in war time don't just dissolve when you get back home. So, like some of the others, Dan and I used to go on training runs together, and we headed into the mountains once or twice a year—but always off the base.

'Right...' Thea hedged. 'But when you were deployed together he never even showed you a photo of me?'

'Having a photo of your wife, or girlfriend, or baby is one thing. But having a photo of your sister... There's no way Dan would have risked the guys seeing a photo of a girl like you. It would have invited attention...comments that a brother wouldn't want to hear about his sister.'

'Oh.'

Thea flushed a deep scarlet as the meaning of his words sank in. He found it surprisingly endearing—a reminder than she had never really appreciated just how stunning she was. Even now.

'Tell me what you thought the first time you met me,' she said. 'On that date we went on together.'

He stiffened. This wasn't a conversation he wanted to be having.

'Please, Ben. I need to hear something...*pleasant*... Everything's gone so very wrong. I just want to hear what you told me that night.'

Ben met her wobbly, pleading gaze. She wanted distraction, a better memory to offer some flicker of consolation at one of the worst times of her life. After the way he'd treated her, surely he owed her that much?

'I thought you were the most beautiful woman I'd ever met,' he said quietly. 'Not just aesthetically, but on the inside, too. You were fun, impetuous...you had a vibrancy about you which was wonderfully infectious to all those around you. You made everyone want to be near you, to be part of your group.'

He'd been on a rare night out with some other officers—at a crowded bar—when Thea had slipped into the space beside him. They'd started talking casually and that had been it—he'd never felt such an inexorable attraction to a woman before. He'd excused himself from his group as soon as he'd been able to, just to spend the rest of the evening in Thea's company.

'Oh...'

She sounded let down, and he knew why. She thought he'd understood her better.

He hesitated, then conceded. 'At least that's what you wanted people to see. But beneath that veil there was a quietness, almost a shyness about you when you thought no one was watching you. Judging you. I assumed it was a defence mechanism you'd created after your parents had died, to stop people asking if you were all right.'

'Really? You *saw* that?'

Her evident pleasure that he'd seen a part of her others had been only too happy to ignore made him want to kiss her and berate her all at the same time. And that was the damned problem.

'So the next day, when you told me we couldn't see each other any more...?' She hiccupped, clearly torn between not wanting to say the words and needing to know the truth. 'You didn't have feelings for me anymore?'

How was he supposed to answer *that*? From the moment they'd met he had been hooked. This spellbinding young woman had persuaded him to take her to a funfair. There had been a small group of them—Thea's friends—but he hadn't even noticed them after the first few minutes. He had only seen Thea.

They'd hurled leather balls at the coconut shy, laughed their way through the hall of mirrors and shared an incredible, intense first kiss at the top of the Ferris wheel.

In most of his life—even much of his childhood—Ben had never felt as happy and free of responsibility as he had that evening with Thea. And he'd known even then that she had an ability to make him fall for her such as no other woman ever had.

And now she wanted to know why he'd walked away from her. What could he say? He owed her something. Perhaps a variation on the truth was the safest option.

'We're just…weren't a good match. I'm sorry, Thea.'

Her body seemed to curl even more into his arms and he felt worse than ever. But it was a necessary lie…no, a half-truth… They *weren't* a good match. Ben could recall tantalising glimpses of a real inner confidence and a love of life, rippling constantly beneath that artificially shimmering, vivacious exterior. He had seen them from the beginning. She was the kind of person who made people feel good, want to bask in her warm glow for ever.

He wished he could be the kind of person who made *her* feel good, who could inspire that hidden side of Thea.

Instead he knew that he was the kind of person who would eventually extinguish that dancing light in her soul. If he was the kind of man his father had been he would drag Thea down, as his mother had been dragged down. What kind a life would that be for a woman like Thea?

He'd known as he'd walked her home that night, wondering at the way she had made him feel about her after just one incredible date, that he needed to walk away from her before he *did* hurt her. But he hadn't been able to. Even as he'd walked up the pathway to her ground-floor flat his head had been telling him one thing whilst his heart had been making plans to take her out the next day. Imagining a future with her.

And then Dan had opened the door and demanded to know what the hell Ben was doing with his sister.

Dan—the guy who'd had his back through countless tours of duty. The buddy who would have given his life for Ben, and for whom Ben would have sacrificed his own.

Only Dan had and Ben hadn't.

So, just like that, the woman he had thought he might actually be able to fall in love with had been off limits. Still, Ben had to wonder whether Dan had been the real reason that he'd walked away from Thea.

Or just the excuse.

He could have fought for her. The thought slid, unbidden, into his mind. But would that have been fair? All the women he'd dated in the past...he'd never felt strongly enough about any of them. With Thea it was different. It had been even from that first meeting. But the closer you were to someone, the more hurt you could cause. Ben had learned that from his parents. If his father had taught him anything, it was never to get close to anyone. Or let them get close to you.

It was a lesson he'd do well to remember with Thea.

Lost in his own dark thoughts, it took Ben a while to realise that she was asleep. He heard her breathing ease and deepen, felt her heartbeat drop to a slow, rhythmic pulse. And for the first time in a long time—with Thea still wrapped in his arms—Ben fell into a deep, restful sleep of his own.

He woke to the sound of an unfamiliar phone alert. A text? An email? Not wanting to wake Thea, Ben squinted through the curtains to the darkness beyond. Years of field experience told him it had to be around four in the morning.

Nevertheless he felt her stir beside him, felt her raise her head up and then reach across him for her phone. He felt the skim of soft breasts and lacy fabric against his bare chest and fought to stop his body's primal reaction. He didn't stand a chance.

Thea froze.

For a moment Ben vacillated. Should he apologise? Leave? She had wanted him there, to comfort her. She had trusted him. Such a base reaction was the ultimate betrayal of that trust. He had no doubt she would consider it as unexpected as it was unwanted.

He was shocked when, instead of scooting off the bed away from him, Thea reached out and touched his face.

'Don't, Thea. It's not a good idea.' He gripped her wrist, stilling it and moving it away from him as he opened his eyes and came face to face with her direct gaze.

She still looked pale, drained; but there was a glint in her eyes which he hadn't been expecting—something he couldn't quite pinpoint.

It held him in her bed, motionless. Part of him knew he should leave. He had promised her this was a marriage on paper only, assured her she could trust him. Still, part of him wanted to stay. He couldn't deny his attraction to her, and all their talk last night had only made it harder to put his feelings for her safely away in their box.

'Why isn't it a good idea?' she whispered, gently twisting her wrist from his loosened grip, slowly returning it to his face.

She traced the outline of the scar which pulled at the corner of his eye. 'Some war wound, huh?' Her voice shook as she spoke,

Memories punched into him. The last time she'd asked that exact question had been on their one and only date, moments before they'd shared their first kiss. Could it only have been six weeks ago? It had been a gentle yet powerful kiss which had rocked him to his foundations in a way he'd never suspected a mere kiss ever could. It was the moment he'd realised he wanted more, so much more, from this woman.

She'd asked him how he'd got it—assuming, as others had done in the past, that it was something to do with the Army. Ben had always been happy to go along with their assumption—not that he'd dated a lot since his career had begun to come first. But instead he'd found himself telling Thea how the scar was a result of running into an open kitchen drawer when he was boy.

In fifteen years he'd barely even spoken to anyone about

his mother. But that night he'd regaled Thea with the story
of how he'd been running away from his half-furious, half-
scared mum, having been found blown halfway across
the room after jamming a kitchen knife into an electrical
socket, trying to retrieve his wedged-in toy soldier.

Thea had been shocked and amused in equal measure,
with no idea of the enormity of what Ben had just done in
telling her something so personal. And now she was trac-
ing his scar and asking him the same question again. Deliberately reminding him of that night.

He felt his willpower slipping.

He snatched his head away, jackknifing his body upright to slide her off him and launching himself sideways
out of the bed. But she slipped her arms around him, stopping him from leaving the bed completely.

'We can't do this, Thea,' he repeated.

If he didn't stop this his self-control would crumble,
and at some point she would come to hate him for letting
this happen She would never forgive him for not staying
strong enough for both of them.

'I don't want to be alone. Not tonight,' she whispered
hoarsely.

Grief was still etched into her expression. He felt torn.
He was supposed to be here to look after her, to support
her—how could he walk out on her now?

He had to get things back to where they'd been a couple
of hours earlier. He could hold her, comfort her, but nothing more was going to happen.

He moved back to the bed and sat down to pull her into
his arms and soothe her, as he had a few hours earlier, but
Thea had other ideas.

Turning her head to his, she pressed her warm mouth
to his skin, kissing his temple, his cheek, the skin inches
from his mouth.

He moved his hand to stay her. 'Stop, Thea. Neither of
us are thinking straight.'

'You're wrong…'

Her shaky voice should have told him more, but he didn't want to hear.

'I know you still want me. And it's precisely because we *aren't* thinking straight that we can do this. We need this. *I* need this. I need oblivion. Take me away from all this. Make me forget the last three weeks. Make me forget everything. If only for a short while.'

'It will still be there afterwards,' he said.

Resisting her touch was taking all his willpower. She was right—he did still want her. Despite the promise he'd made to himself six weeks ago, never to go near Thea again, he hadn't stopped wanting her or thinking about her. She had haunted his dreams.

'Just make me forget for a moment. Please, Ben, can you do that?'

She touched him again and his mental grip slipped further. He shouldn't give in, but he was losing control, his head was spinning. Grief, guilt, lust—all mingled together with his lack of sleep over the last month, and Ben struggled to pick his way through the tangle of emotions.

As if sensing his weakening resolve, Thea slid hesitant fingers under the waistband of his boxer shorts, looking to him as if for compliance. He should stand his ground, tell her that she was still grieving and scared and confused, that she didn't know what she was doing.

Except it seemed as if she knew exactly what she was doing. She seemed to know what she wanted and just what effect she was having on him. And, as she'd already pointed out, she knew only too well how much he wanted her.

With a slight dip of his head he conveyed his acquiescence, sucking in deep breath as Thea slid his boxers off him and surveyed every inch of him. Then, almost shyly, she took his hand and moved it to her breast. Her nipple was hard against his palm.

The effect was instantaneous. Pushing her back into

the middle of the bed, Ben moved to cover her body with his, and as she arched slightly to meet him every inch of their bodies was pressed into delicious contact. Slowly he lowered his mouth to hers, to claim it as his own, but she squirmed slightly beneath him.

'I don't need the niceties,' she said, flushing red at her boldness. 'I just need you to take me. To make me forget.'

Ben scanned her face. It must have taken some courage for her to say that. He hesitated. Since he'd met her, kissed her, six weeks ago, she had danced into his late-night fantasies, but this wasn't the way he'd imagined their first time to be. Still, there would be plenty of time for languid, indulgent exploration of each other's bodies the next time— and the time after that. If immediate release was what she wanted now, this time, then he wasn't objecting. He just wanted Thea—to touch her, to claim her.

He slid his knee between her legs, gliding his hands over her skin.

'Open for me,' he murmured, revelling in her immediate compliance, sliding his fingers between her legs and finding her hot and wet.

'God…' He gave a guttural groan. 'You're going to be my undoing.'

She gasped as he dipped inside her, finding her clit and flicking back and forth, knowing just the right amount of pressure to elicit a moan of pleasure from her. But before he could continue her hand pushed down between their bodies, her fingers latching around his wrist as she pushed him away, wrapping her legs around him instead and shifting her body so it was central to his.

The tip of his erection skimmed her damp heat and he heard another low moan. It took him a moment to realise it was his own voice.

'No niceties, Ben. Remember?' Thea muttered.

'This is all you want?' Ben asked. Holding back when he was this close was almost unbearable, but he had to be sure.

'It's all I want,' she confirmed, burying her head in his shoulder.

Unable to hold back any longer, he pushed inside her, feeling her stretch around him, tilting her pelvis up slightly to draw him in deeper and deeper. Her arms slid around his back, holding on to him as he rocked inside her. He knew he was close—six weeks of almost nightly dreams of Thea, and none of them had come close to the reality. And this wasn't even their best. But, if the way she was tightening around him was anything to go by, he wasn't the only one close to the edge.

Resting his weight on one arm as he continued his relentless rhythm, he reached for her thigh with his other arm, hooking his hand under her knee and locking her leg around his back. The action opened her up just a fraction more, and Ben heard her little sounds of pleasure as he thrust deeper, harder. Then she was arching up again, her breath quickening, and as she orgasmed she tightened around him—only moments before he felt his own climax crashing over him. His back stiffened and he groaned, spilling inside her, barely able to think but careful to hold his weight off her.

'Ben...?' she whispered, almost expectantly.

Was she waiting for him to say something? For a split second he wished he was good with words—wished he could tell her how he felt right now. Instead he froze, and reality hit him.

This was *exactly* why he'd needed to stay away from her. He would always be shutting her out, and she would always be fighting for him to let her in. He would never be able to give her what she needed. He was useless.

It was only when he raised himself up to look at her that he saw the tears spilling from her eyes. Horrified, he slipped out of her, rolling onto his side to pull her into his arms.

Thea resisted.

This was what he'd been afraid of.

'This was one of the three most horrific days of my life...' She stumbled over her words.

'I know.' What more could he say?

'I just thought it would make it better. Us. Together. Just this once.'

'And it didn't?' He felt sick. Of course it hadn't. Hadn't he told himself this would happen?

She shook her head, the tears coming faster now.

'If anything, it's made it worse.'

Moving quickly off her bed, he searched for his boxers. Found them. Slid them on as quickly as he could.

He had known she wasn't thinking straight. But *he* should have known better—saved her from herself. Instead he had taken shameless advantage of her. All because his own lust for her had let him believe her when she'd said it was what she wanted.

His brain searched for something to say—anything which would express how very sorry he was. Nothing came. How could it?

The past—*their* past—his emotional distance...it was all bound to catch up with them sooner or later. Perhaps it was best that it was sooner. Before anything more happened between them. He needed to get away—put some space between them before he hurt her any more than he already had.

'You're leaving?' she asked flatly.

'I think it's for the best.' *So why did the words stick in his throat?*

'What now?' Her sad, wary eyes sought his.

He hesitated by the door. 'My compassionate leave is almost over. I'll be shipping out soon anyway.'

'So we go back to the original marriage agreement?' she asked urgently, as if seeking that security at the very least.

He wanted to say no, to tell her that he couldn't go back to anything after what had just happened between them.

He wanted to tell her that he wanted more from her, from their marriage. But what had happened between them had only cemented his fear that she was already under his skin and he'd never want to let her go. He owed her more than that. He was no more able to be the kind of man she needed now than he had been six weeks ago. On top of which, his guilt at not being someone she could trust weighed heavily on him. Until he was able to make amends for that he could never ask more of her. So he owed her what he'd originally promised.

'Yes,' he confirmed at length. 'We go back to the original deal.'

She nodded once—a sad bob of her head.

Before he could say anything more—wreck things any further—Ben yanked the door open and escaped into the hallway. Forget a few more days. There was no way he could stay in this house with Thea for even one more night. He needed to get out of here. *Now.*

CHAPTER THREE

Present day

BEN WATCHED THE interns shuffle out of his side room. The habitual idolising smiles they gave whenever they saw him set Ben's teeth on edge.

'They annoy you, don't they?' Thea asked, suddenly appearing at his door.

He ruthlessly ignored the kick of pleasure at her presence. She shouldn't have to be here. He wasn't her problem.

'They treat me like some kind of…'

'Hero?' Thea smiled.

'I'm not a hero.' Ben ground out the words.

'Two weeks ago you were caught by two IEDs. The first one severed your left arm, yet you still managed to drag your men to safety before getting caught by a second IED. Geez, Ben, you were pinned under a Land Rover with a suspected crushed spine—it could have left you in a wheelchair for the rest of your life.'

'It *could have* but it didn't,' Ben growled. 'They couldn't tell because of the swelling so they suspected the worst. They were wrong,' Ben refuted flatly. 'It turned out I'm fine. I just need to get out of here.'

'You're hardly *fine*,' Thea scoffed. 'You still suffered contusions of the spinal cord. You were lucky not to sever it. Not to mention you've dislocated and shattered a whole raft of vertebrae which have had to be pinned and bolted. Oh, and did I mention the replantation of your arm?'

'Really?' Ben arched an eyebrow at her. 'I hadn't noticed—other than the fact that my left arm is now two centimetres shorter than my right arm.'

If he'd thought to intimidate her then he'd thought wrong. If anything, she looked almost amused.

'Then you're damned lucky. I saw a girl last year whose right arm was not only severed, but crushed. By the time they cut away the damaged tissue and bone her arm ended up twelve centimetres shorter than the other. This year she underwent bone-lengthening surgery and she'll be over the moon if she reduces that to a two-centimetre difference. And did I say that she's right-handed, like you, but unlike you *she's* now had to learn to be left-handed?'

'Then, like I said before,' he pointed out, 'I'm fine.'

'You're lucky, Ben, but you're not fine. And pretending you are is only making you push yourself far, *far* harder than anyone else is comfortable with.'

Before he could respond Thea advanced into the room, ticking off her fingers as she counted the days.

'Let me break this down for you, Ben. Days one, two and three you were operated on, flown here, and put into traction until the swelling could go down and they could better assess the damage to your spine. That happened on day six. By day seven they were able to operate. By day eight you already had sensation in your lower limbs and were able to move your left big toe on command. Day nine your left toes and your right big toe. By day ten you could move both feet. By day eleven you could lift your left leg above the bed, and day twelve your right leg—'

'Is there any point to this?' Ben interrupted.

He shifted irritably in the wingback chair. He hated being in this thing almost as much as he hated being in the damned wheelchair. The sooner Thea left, the better.

'Yes,' she replied, unflustered. 'It's now day eighteen. By rights you should be up and about in a wheelchair, and you *might* be able to take a few steps around your room with the aid of a frame. Instead of which you're pushing yourself around in gruelling laps of the hospital like you think you're some kind of superhero.'

'I do *not* think I'm some kind of superhero.'

'Really? Then let me check your chart.'

She was right about one thing, though. He *was* desperate to get out of the room, away from Thea, and push his broken body to try another circuit of the floor. Even the pain was a welcome distraction from the nightmares which haunted his darkest thoughts. Nightmares of explosions and of IEDs, of flying debris and vehicles. The old nightmares too, of Daniel screaming out to him. And now, this last fortnight, inexplicable new nightmares—of Thea, looking on as he lay helpless and weak. In his nightmares he could never work out whether her expression was one of satisfaction or sympathy. Vindication that he'd finally got his comeuppance? Or pity?

No, the pain was good—it meant that he was alive.

So he forced himself to stay still, trapped as he was in the too-soft seat, and tried to the let Thea's words wash over him. He studiously averted his gaze from the detestable hospital bed—in which he tried to spend the very least time he possibly could—and attempted to conceal his frustration.

'Aha, nothing to indicate a problem on your read-outs. However...' She glanced up at him before reading the notes. *"'Visual assessment suggests breathing seems shallow, cheeks flushed and feverish—query possibility of infection.'"*

'It's wrong,' Ben dismissed it.

'Of course it is,' Thea snapped. 'Since you know, and I know, and fortunately even Dr Fields knows enough to note that any potentially concerning visual indicators are nothing more than a result of the fact that you got up at around five a.m., and then spent the last couple of hours pushing beyond your body's limits in completing circuits of the hospital before hobbling here—probably in considerable pain—to beat Dr Fields and his interns back on to the ward before they started their rounds.'

'It's called recovery.' He gritted his teeth. 'I need to push my body to help it heal.'

'You need to *rest*!' Thea cried out. 'Ben, in all serious-ness, you have done *incredibly* well—in no small part due to your grit and determination. It usually takes five weeks to get where you are now, and you've done it in under three. But you need to take things easy.'

'The sooner I recover, the sooner I can get out of here.'

'Ben, you *have* to know that's not going to happen. Not whilst you still refuse to come home with me. You need someone to take care of you during your recuperation.'

'I don't need *anyone*,' Ben snarled. 'Least of all you.'

He didn't want to hurt her, but it was the only way he could think of to chase her away. She shouldn't be here—he wasn't her responsibility. Not when he'd treated her the way he had. But, really, what choice had he had?

There's always a choice. The thought crept into his head before he could stop it. *You just made the wrong one.*

'That's why I need to push my body. Recover. Then I won't need to be discharged into anyone's care,' he spat out.

'That isn't going to happen, Major.' Dr Fields strode into the room, one of his interns by his side.

Dammit, that blasted smile of adulation again.

'Ben, this isn't just about your physical recovery. Even if your rehabilitation continues on this fast track you've put yourself on—and I highly doubt that it will, since I think you're pushing yourself far too hard and will end up doing your body more harm than good—I would still need to know you had someone to stay with during the last part of your recuperation. Someone to support you, talk to you, observe you and make sure they're on hand if there happen to be any unforeseen complications.'

'If you're talking PTSD, Doc, just come out and say it.' Ben shook his head. 'I'm fine.'

'You might not want to admit it...' the doctor spoke gently '...but the nightmares which wake you in the night, have you screaming out in a cold sweat, are a symptom of PTSD. It's still relatively mild at this stage, and only natural after all you've been through, but the longer you refuse to deal with it, the worse it will get.'

'There are men out there who have suffered a lot worse than me,' Ben growled, not wanting to be having this conversation. 'Buddies of mine who lost limbs or didn't even make it. I'm already back on my feet. I've nothing to complain about.'

'Which is the problem.' Dr Fields sighed. 'Still, we'll save that for another day.'

No, they wouldn't. Ben gave an almost imperceptible shake of his head. *He was fine, even if he didn't deserve to be. But he needed to get out of here.*

His eyes slid to Thea. For all her bravado now, he could still remember her standing by his bedside in those first few days, her face white with fear and concern for a man she hadn't seen in five years. He clenched his fists; she'd been dragged into this out of some misplaced sense of obligation but it had nothing to do with her. There was no way he was about to let her take responsibility for his care. Her unfailing loyalty was her downfall.

He could only imagine how much she must have resented being summoned here. How much she must hate him—dragging her into a marriage in order to fulfil his own need to honour his promise to her brother. Only to give in to his baser desires, his long-standing attraction to her. So what if they had both shared the attraction at one time? He'd had no right—it hadn't been part of the plan. And, anyway, what kind of man bedded his dead best friend's grief-stricken sister?

'Ultimately, Ben, your body still has a lot of healing to do, and I am concerned that you're driving yourself too hard. You need to back up a little, or you risk doing permanent damage.'

'I hear you, Doc.' Ben nodded flatly. *No chance. He was out of here as soon as they all left him alone.*

Dr Fields turned away from Ben to the intern. 'Dr Thompson—since Major Abrams isn't feeling compliant, I suggest you run those tests after all. Time-consuming, yet non-costly,' he added pointedly. 'I may not be able to stop Major Abrams from destroying the body I worked so hard to repair, but I *can* slow him down. At least for a few hours.'

'Really, Doc? Pointless tests?' challenged Ben.

'They aren't pointless if they stop you from hauling your butt out of here the minute we walk out the door for another set of exhausting laps. Now, Dr Abrams—' Ben started, and then realised that Dr Fields was addressing Thea. 'Have you got a moment?'

Ben resisted the uncharacteristic compulsion to get up and throw the chair out of the window. For a start, he doubted he'd have the strength. And secondly he never let his temper get the better of him. He never let *any* emotion get the better of him—hadn't his father always drilled into him the need to keep a tight, unrelenting control over all his emotions as all times? He'd be ashamed of Ben if he knew how his son had used Thea five years ago. Not that his father had ever been proud of him—even when he'd followed in the Colonel's footsteps into the army.

Ben shut down the familiar sense of failure, but it had already got a grip, and as the intern began his nonsensical tests Ben couldn't deny that part of him was grateful for the excuse to take a break—if only for an hour of rest. It was probably the same part of him which was finding it so damned painful to put one foot in front of the other as he shuffled along at such an interminably slow pace.

Weakness, he thought with disgust, and his father's words echoed in his ears. *Weakness has no place here.*

* * *

Ben grunted with effort as he executed a one-armed pull-up out of the wingback chair and into the wheelchair which would allow him off the ward without attracting attention. Ever since Thea had visited yesterday that intern had held him hostage, running unnecessary test after test. He hadn't managed to get out once, and it had left him feeling irritable.

Yet he couldn't deny that his body felt stronger than ever after a full twenty hours of rest. Maybe today was the day to push himself to walk outside in the fresh air. Once he was outside, in the quieter areas of the hospital grounds, he could discard the unwanted lump of metal and force his body not to be so weak. Dr Fields was wrong. He needed to push harder, not less.

He propelled the wheelchair along strongly with his good arm, only stopping once he'd reached the peaceful gardens outside and found a quiet spot. With a deep breath he pulled himself to an unassisted standing position. So much for a walk. He didn't think he could even take a step. Thank goodness no one could see him like this—weak as a kitten and utterly tragic.

'So now you're trying to kill yourself trying to walk around outside the hospital, without even a wall to lean on?'

His head jerked up. It was an effort to stay upright, but he'd be damned if he fell over in front of *her*. In front of anyone.

He lashed out before he could stop himself. 'What the hell are you doing here? Are you following me?'

Thea blanched visibly at his hostility and he immediately felt ashamed of himself. Yesterday she'd been so strong, so unintimidated, he had forgotten how easily undermined she could be. The last thing he wanted was to hurt her, yet he had to stay resolute. Thea was only here because the Army had contacted her as his next of kin—as his wife.

His wife. The words echoed around Ben's head, taunting him.

For five years there had been no contact between them, and these sure as hell weren't the circumstances in which Ben would ever have chosen to have her back in his life. When he was helpless and unable to provide for her...to protect her. A wave of self-loathing washed over him. He wasn't even a proper man any more. Just a shell of a man who couldn't walk without leaning heavily on a wall, a rail, a walking frame.

Pathetic, he thought scornfully.

He needed Thea to leave. *Now.* And surely she *wanted* to leave, deep down? She couldn't want to be with him now. No one could. He had to convince Thea that her duty was done, that he was fine and that he didn't need her. Then she could leave, get on with her life.

He steeled himself. 'Hell, Thea, can't you see that I don't want you here?'

'I don't understand what I've done to make you hate me so much.'

As fast as the anger had arrived, it disappeared. *Hate her?* What on earth made her think that? If anything, it should be the other way around.

Suddenly he felt exhausted. He didn't want to fight with her any more. He just wanted her to feel free to go back to her own life whilst he concentrated on his recovery.

'I've never hated you.' Ben spoke quietly. 'But our marriage was never meant to be anything more than on paper. You shouldn't be here now—this isn't your responsibility. I was just trying to make you see that.'

'If you don't want me here, then answer me something.'

'Answer you what?' he asked, wondering why he felt as though he was walking into some carefully set trap.

'Why am I still listed on your Army paperwork as your next of kin?'

Ben felt his breathing stop, before exhaling with a

whoosh of air. So he was right—she *was* only here under obligation, because the Army had called her. She resented him for it, and he couldn't blame her.

'I left you on the Army paperwork because we were married. If I'd put down someone else as my next of kin it would have raised questions.'

'I see.'

Something flashed across her face, but it was gone before he could identify it.

He'd also left her on it so that she would always have a direct means to get in touch with him if she ever needed his help. He'd even hoped she would—especially in those first months after their wedding night. After all, they hadn't used protection. He supposed it was a blessing that nothing had ever come of it; in his experience an absent soldier never made a good dad. And yet he suspected a tiny part of him had once hoped otherwise. Not that he could say that now.

The silence hung between them.

'Now I see that it was a mistake,' he ground out eventually.

A mistake. Was that really how he thought of her?

Thea felt the nausea churn in her stomach, as it had been doing practically every day since she'd heard about Ben's accident.

She watched him edge painstakingly to the rock wall across the hidden courtyard, and resisted the urge to leap down and ram his wheelchair under his backside, just to stop him from punishing his body.

She spotted a movement out of the corner of her eye—it was the man who had been outside Ben's hospital room that first day. She'd thought he was some kind of Army specialist, but now she wasn't so sure. She'd seen him a few more times over the last few weeks, always observing but never making any direct contact with Ben. Perhaps

he was some kind of counsellor—someone Ben could talk
to. Someone who might be able to understand this irratio-
nal need Ben seemed to have to push his body to breaking
point—and maybe beyond.

The first time she'd seen Ben in the wheelchair she'd
felt a laugh of disbelief roll around her chest. It had been a
welcome light-hearted moment in days of frustrating ig-
norance and gloom. Only Ben Abrams could have engen-
dered a posse of men from his unit marching down to the
hospital to present their hero commander with a racing
chair which had once belonged to a former Paralympic
basketball champion.

And only Ben would have hurtled around the corridors
in it the following week as though he was in a rally car on
a racing circuit, pushing his one good arm past its limits.

Even she, who was impervious to him now—or at least
ought to be—hadn't been able to ignore the fact that the
simple white tee shirt he'd worn had done little to hide the
shifts and ripples of the already well-honed muscles which
had glistened, to the delight of several of the medical staff,
covered with a perfect sheen of sweat.

She could still remember the feel of that solid chest
against her body…the sensation of completeness as he
moved inside her.

*You, my girl, have all the resistance of a chocolate
fireguard.* She shook her head in frustration. Hadn't she
learned anything from that night? Despite his warnings,
despite his resistance, she had pushed and pushed until
Ben had ended up hurting her—more than she could have
thought possible.

Yet here she was. And she might have come for closure,
but he was already shaking up her emotions. It was difficult to keep hating a real-life hero who was prepared to
sacrifice his own life for others time and again. Not just on
an everyday basis, or even after Daniel had died, but when
he'd been so very badly injured himself in that bomb blast.

According to some of the neighbourhood wives, all the Army convoys used frequency-jamming devices—which meant that the enemy who had detonated the IED which had caught Ben's patrol had to have been close by. Close enough to potentially have had a shooter to take individuals out.

Ben would have known that too. With all his training it would have been one of the first things he had realised. But instead of taking cover he'd stepped up anyway, to save the lives of five of his men. By rights he shouldn't be alive.

She had to admire this man who was so hell-bent on fighting his way back to full health, who refused to sit back and wallow in self-pity. Even his frustration, his anger now, was because he refused to accept the limitations his body was imposing on him.

She just wished he could let his guard down, even once, and let her in. But he never would. She wondered if he even knew how to.

There was no doubt that Ben's sheer grit had helped him achieve in a few weeks what other patients far more fortunate than him were still fighting to attain after months. She might have known Ben Abrams would be a rare breed… What was it her brother had once told her the men called Ben? Ah, yes, 'the Mighty Abs'. And indeed he was—by name and nature.

He even garnered attention in this place—not just as a soldier, but as a man. She wondered how much female attention he'd enjoyed over the last five years. It was none of her business, she knew that, and yet she couldn't seem to silence the niggling question.

Giving in to temptation, Thea allowed herself a lazy assessment of the man she had once thought herself in love with. Five years on and there were obvious differences, but he still resembled the young man she had known—if only briefly. Despite the dark rings around his eyes—testament to his recent experience—there was no mistaking that he was lethally handsome. Not *pretty-boy* handsome—he'd never been that—but a deep, interesting, arresting handsome.

The nose which had been broken in the field a few times only enhanced the dangerous appeal he already oozed, and the scar by his eyebrow snagged at his eye, lending him a devil-may-care attitude. She remembered kissing that scar. The feel of his skin under her lips. The glide of her hands down that infamous torso. In her naivety she'd believed that if he gave in to her once, just once, he would realise that they could start again…redefine their relationship.

Sheer folly.

Now, at twenty-six, she understood what Ben had known all along. Things between them would never have worked. He was too entrenched in his ways and she was too idealistic. Still, even if she had realised that one night would be their only night, she wouldn't have changed it—even to spare herself the pain. But she *would* have taken her time that night. She hadn't been a virgin, but at twenty-one she hadn't had a wealth of experience either. She'd spent the last five years imagining how it would have felt if she'd let Ben do all the things to her he'd wanted to, let herself explore him more…

Heat suffused her body and, embarrassed, Thea dragged her mind from such inappropriate ponderings. Her emotions had been all over the place since she'd seen him again.

Because you still haven't told him your painful secret, goaded a little voice. She closed her mind but it refused to be silenced. *What about the baby you lost? Ben's baby?*

As long as he'd been away she'd been able to convince herself that it wasn't the sort of thing that could be explained over the phone. But now that he was back she no longer had that excuse. She'd have to tell him before he left again. But not now—and not here.

'Anyway, I'm not following you,' she said abruptly. 'Yes-

terday I was visiting you, but today I'm working in the area.
I'm on my lunch break.'

'You work here?'

'The scrubs didn't give it away?'

Ben frowned. 'You were in your final year of medicine at uni when I left. Then you were going to be a junior
house officer. I thought you wanted to go into paediatrics
after rotations? That your goal was Great Ormond Street?'

She felt an unexpected rush of pleasure that he remembered. It shouldn't matter. But it did.

'It was. But then Daniel died and everything changed.'
She shrugged, seeing the flash of sorrow in his eyes before
his face closed against her, as she remembered it doing a
decade earlier when she'd spoken her brother's name. Just
another reminder of the fact that he could never open up
to her.

'I realised I was better in trauma. Daniel had taught me
some stuff over the years—techniques you guys use out
in war zones which had yet to filter down to Civvy Street.
I was able to adapt those things into my own work, so I
started to gain quite a reputation. Before long I was getting offers to go and learn from Army trauma doctors who
were coming back from Afghanistan. The more I learned,
the better I became, and the more offers I got.'

'So now you work here? Nice scrubs... Blue always
was your colour,' he said without thinking. The conversation topic had momentarily given them common ground.

'Actually, I work with the Air Ambulance as a trauma
doctor. I just happen to be on secondment here at the moment.'

He saw through the excuse immediately, and the moment of connection between them disappeared as he glowered at her. 'You're playing with your career to stay here
and check up on me?'

Dammit—she hadn't wanted him to realise. She'd been

lucky that the Air Ambulance had been so understanding from the moment she'd told them about Ben last month.

'I'm one of the doctors for the Air Ambulance. I don't *play* with my career,' she objected. 'They have set up a temporary exchange programme with one of the hospital-based trauma doctors for me.'

'Are you that good?' He looked impressed.

'Yes.' Thea nodded proudly and offered a cheeky grin. Typical of Ben to cut to the chase, and she wasn't about to disappoint him with false modesty. She was proud of all she'd achieved—especially after losing Daniel and Ben, albeit for very different reasons. 'I *am* good, as it happens.'

She'd worked hard for her achievements, and her past had driven her on—including Ben's abandonment.

'There'll always be more to learn—new procedures, research progress… That's the nature of medicine—you know that. But, yes, I'm one of the top in my field.'

'I'm pleased for you,' Ben acknowledged, and the sincerity in his tone gave her an unexpectedly warm glow.

She had been setting money aside ever since her first decent job, and now had enough to pay Ben back every bit of money he'd ever given her for her education. But something warned her that now wasn't the time to mention it. Somehow they seemed to have struck the beginnings of an uneasy truce, and she wasn't about to jeopardise it.

'So, you've been here every day?'

'When I'm working here. Sorry, Ben, I don't have time to come and visit you all the time.'

Had her nose just grown about a foot? She had been surprised that he hadn't informed Dr Fields that they were estranged and got him to force her to stay away. But then, that would have entailed talking to a stranger about his private life.

Thea watched as he tried not to let her see he was leaning on the rock wall for support. The nurses had told her he'd long been refusing any pain medication, claiming it would prevent him from being able to tell whether his body was healing or not. She wasn't convinced—there had to be more to it than that. Still, it was little wonder that his brain was hazy if he was dealing with that level of pain. If so, was this her perfect opportunity to convince him that he should be discharged into her care?

Apprehension rippled through her. If she was honest, she wasn't sure she wanted him in her home again—it threatened to raise too many unanswered questions. She'd thought Ben was firmly in her past until she'd received that nightmare phone call a few weeks ago. Then she'd realised she needed closure. But the way he had her emotions scattering all over the place scared her. She couldn't afford to let him get under her skin again.

But if he needed someone looking out for him for the next few months then she owed him that much after all he'd done for her. Besides, as the cottage was part of Army married quarters, technically it was as much *his* house as it was hers.

'You've got your hospital stay and your initial rehab stay. After that you'll have a long-term rehab stay—*or* you can choose to come home with me so that I can help you through your recovery.'

'So that you can keep tabs on me, you mean?'

'Yes, if you like.'

No point in denying it.

'Look, Ben, you're going to push yourself—we both know that. Hell, the whole hospital knows that. But they won't discharge you to live on your own. They have a duty of care to make sure that someone is around.'

'Thea, I don't want to have this conversation with you.'

'Well, frankly, I don't want to have this conversation with you either,' she bit back.

He'd never listen to her if she buckled at his first objection. She'd been preparing her line of argument for the last week.

'Ben, the situation is ridiculous. It's your house too—married quarters because you're an officer. Don't you think that people are suspicious that they've never seen you there? Did you know that I've had to pretend to go away, stay in hotels, just to pretend we're together when you're on leave? If you don't come home now, being this injured, you're going to open us up to an investigation.'

She shrugged. Maybe that was what he wanted. For the Army finally to realise. Take the house away. Force them to face up to their sham marriage and divorce? She wasn't sure.

'I'm sure we can live there together on a temporary basis...*separately*.' She licked her lips, forcefully blocking any more memories of their night together in that house.

'Separately. Of course,' Ben echoed.

His voice sounded unexpectedly hoarse, as if his mind had taken him to the same place hers had. Which was ridiculous, she knew, and fanciful. She doubted Ben *ever* thought about that night, or else he did and cringed at the way she'd thrown herself at him.

Yes, she definitely needed closure.

'Consider it, Ben,' she pressed on. 'You gave me a home, and you funded me so I didn't have to drop out of medicine at uni and take some waitressing job, or something, just to keep a roof over my head. Do you know how many people out there have the smarts but could never pay for the education *you* paid for—for me?'

'You achieved this by yourself,' Ben growled. 'Your success is nothing to do with me.'

'You're wrong,' Thea shook her head, wondering why he suddenly looked so angry again. 'I feel I owe you. If you come back home we can stay out of each other's way, but you can recover at your own pace and get back to the Army. Because that's your goal, right?'

His face said it all, and it was as if her heart plummeted to the uneven flags underfoot. What was it that drove him so that he refused to take care of himself and let his body recover? He seemed so hell-bent on getting back to the Army, being redeployed as fast as he could.

Or was it just that he was desperate to get away from her? Again.

She shook her head and faced Ben down.

'Fine. So you come home, recover properly, and then you're free to get on with your life. And I can get on with mine knowing that I owe you nothing. From that point on my successes *will* be my own. Deal?'

She waited, wondering what lunacy had made her think that Ben would agree.

Still, she couldn't help pushing... 'Deal?'

'I'll think about it,' Ben rumbled at length.

'Think hard,' she bit out.

He had at least four more months of recovery and procedures in the hospital—although at the rate Ben was going he'd be out much sooner than that—so she had some more time to work on him. But today was a start. He might not have wanted her to be his wife, but after supporting her financially all these years she owed him something. And at least he wasn't refusing outright any more.

CHAPTER FOUR

'So, HERE WE ARE…*home*.'

Whether she meant her home, his home or theirs, Ben wasn't quite sure. But, despite the overly cheery demeanour, the slight catch to her voice, which she had tried so hard to hide, reassured him that she was finding this whole thing as awkward as he was.

He looked up at the familiar and yet alien house. It had been five years—hardly any wonder that he felt almost apprehensive about going inside. He stood there, his one solitary bag at his feet, and stared at climbing roses he didn't remember, a freshly painted fence which was so well bedded into the grass it had clearly been first built a few years ago. Even the evening sun seemed to be in on the act, picture-perfect as it set over the roof.

This wasn't his home. This was Thea's home. And he felt like an intruder.

What the hell was he doing here?

'Ben?' Thea walked over to him, holding out his walking cane.

He gave a single, sharp shake of his head.

'I don't need it.'

'Ben. Don't be too proud.' She reached for his bag. 'You've achieved in three months what it takes most patients five or six to achieve. But you still have a way to go.'

He stayed her hand and she jerked her head sharply to look at him.

'At least let me carry it for you.'

'Thanks, but I can manage,' he spoke quietly.

'Ben...'

'I can manage, Thea,' he repeated firmly, softening his words with a smile.

The hospital might not have been prepared to discharge him unless he had someone to take care of him, but he'd be damned if he'd let his presence interfere with Thea's life—even for a moment.

Slinging his bag over his shoulder and ignoring the flash of pain—less pain now...more an intense discomfort from his arm—he urged his reluctant legs to follow Thea through the door.

Was it really only five years earlier that he had handed the keys of this house over to Thea? Both of them had been in a daze of grief and shock, but he recalled muttering something about decorating it any way she liked, since he spent so much time away on back-to-back tours.

Even through the fug, he remembered he had seen the place through her eyes. Her small flat had been full of colour, and life and memories. The Army cottage had been bland mimosa walls, brown carpets and standard issue grilled-lightshades. Much like his Officer's accommodation in barracks had been before marrying Evie. Not to mention his abject lack of any personal effects.

That was something Ben had picked up as a kid. His father had loathed ornaments—dust-harbourers, he'd called them. Not even a photo of Ben's beloved mother had been allowed, because of the dust which would collect on the glass. And Ben had become accustomed to bareness, nowhere ever felt like a home—it was always just a place to lay his head.

Thea had changed the cottage. Army accommodation or not, this was like a completely different place. The walls were a warm colour and she had replaced the carpets with engineered floorboards, which made the place look clean and fresh, and somehow bigger.

'New curtains…nice…' He gestured, feeling he ought to say something.

The curtains were held back from the windows with pretty metal ties and light flooded into the downstairs room, bouncing off the two couches in the centre, one a vibrant purple and one a rich red. In his head he knew it ought to clash, but it didn't—it all came together beautifully. She'd injected colour and a real sense of fun into the place.

His sense of unease grew.

It felt like a proper home. Not girly or overly feminine, but somewhere he could instantly feel comfortable. And that made him feel disquieted. Yet what would he have preferred? That everything would be as it was the day he'd walked out? With boxes still in the hallway?

Whatever he'd expected, this wasn't it. He didn't like the way it welcomed him…suited him.

But Thea definitely wasn't the same girl he'd left. She had grown up a lot in five years, and her home, like her, was sophisticated and yet still with that irrepressible sense of fun and a zest for life. He was glad. His one regret had been that his actions might have crushed that vibrancy out of her. It was good to see that in some ways she was still the same Thea who had once so captivated him.

And that was what was most worrying.

'Um…do you want to sit down?' Thea asked abruptly. 'You're making the place look…'

'Look what?' he prompted uneasily. This was going to be even harder than he'd feared if she was so used to living alone that she thought he'd disturb everything in the place just by setting foot in it. 'Unsightly?'

'Not unsightly…'

Thea chewed the inside of her lip nervously. It was a trait he suddenly remembered from long ago.

'Ben, we're not going to get very far if you think I feel you're getting in the way. It's just…you're kind of filling up the door frame.' She wrinkled her nose, her cheeks flushing slightly. 'It makes the cottage look a little…small all of a sudden.'

'Right,' Ben acknowledged. *What was that supposed to mean?*

'It's a compliment,' she offered uncertainly.

'Oh, right. Thanks, then.' He tried to smile, but it felt taut on his cheeks. It hadn't *sounded* very complimentary. It had sounded definitively put out. 'Well, I'm pretty beat… it's been a long day. Mind if I hit whichever room is mine and freshen up?'

'Sure. I've set up the dining room.'

'Sorry?'

'The dining room.' She gesticulated, as though he might have forgotten where it was.

'Is there something wrong with the actual bedrooms?' He hadn't meant for his voice to sound so menacing, but he caught the nervous flicker of her eyes.

She licked her lips. 'I thought it you might prefer to avoid the stairs. You're healing well, and I know you're walking normally on level ground again, but the physios did say that stairs could still be a problem for a few months. I've ordered a temporary stairlift, so you can get to the bathroom, plus there's a downstairs toilet and—'

'Stop right there.' He held his hand up. If Thea thought him incapable of getting upstairs by himself, then she was mistaken. 'I'm not staying down here. I'll get myself upstairs and I'll sleep in a proper bedroom, shower in a proper bathroom. And you can cancel any damned stairlift. Now, which room can I use?'

'You're being ridiculous. You still need to recover.'

'Which room, Thea?'

She *harrumphed* in displeasure, and despite his frustration he thought it was so old-Thea-like that it almost made him smile.

'Fine. You can take your old room. I left it for you in case you ever decided to return.'

Ben frowned at the unexpectedly pointed comment. He felt as though he was missing something. When would Thea *ever* have wanted him to return? He narrowed his eyes at her, but she was already turning around, busying herself with rearranging the cushions of the couch. No, he had to be imagining it.

He inclined his head—redundantly, since she still had her back to him—and ducked out of the pretty living room. Climbing the stairs was still harder than he would like, especially with the added weight of his bag. He'd tried a short, slow jog around the hospital grounds the other night. Even though it had hurt like hell, it was still easier than climbing stairs, which tugged at the incision site on his back.

He reached the top landing gratefully. Would his room would be unchanged? As he'd left it? Did he want it to be? Or would he prefer it if Thea had worked her magic in there too, whisking away the memories of that last night together? Memories which had danced into his dreams over the years until he'd finally stuffed them away, locking them out for good.

He passed Thea's bedroom door and paused, standing motionless in the hallway for a moment. If only things had been different. If only *he* had been different.

But he wasn't different.

Shaking off the feeling, Ben moved to his own door and opened it. He was pleasantly surprised. Apart from the fact that Thea had taken away the old carpet, and sanded and varnished the beautiful floorboards underneath, as well as giving the place a dust and polish and a lick of paint, the place looked familiar. Fresh bedding lay folded on the clean mattress, and the empty drawer units smelled citrusy clean. When he opened the storage closet in the corner of the room he almost jumped as one of his old kit bags tumbled out. He'd go through that later.

Busying himself putting his few items away and grabbing a shower was unexpectedly satisfying, and it occurred to Ben that part of the problem was that he wasn't used to having nothing to do. Normally, if he wasn't deployed, he'd be on some adventure trip, learning new skills or honing old ones, or maybe planning training exercises and evaluating his men.

He felt bored—as if he was stagnating. He missed the exhilaration of successful trauma surgery, and his active mind was finding other areas to divert itself into. Dangerous areas. Like remembering their one night together. He couldn't afford to do that. However he tried to spin it, he'd betrayed her trust, and he wasn't the right man for Thea.

The dynamic between them had been irreversibly altered, and since a romantic relationship wasn't an option after he'd left her that night he'd bunked at a mate's house until he'd been shipped out. He'd been doing back-to-back tours ever since. Punishing duties in dangerous regions. Either he would pay off his dues or be killed.

His face twisted bitterly. Neither had happened.

Sometimes, in the beginning, Ben had wondered how things would have turned out if Daniel hadn't been his buddy. Hadn't been Thea's brother. Hadn't died. If he and Thea had been able to be together, would the whirlwind of that night have been sustainable? Would they have had the chance to explore a proper relationship slowly? In their own time? Maybe even got married for real?

He shook his head, as if to rid it of such pointless musings. Thea needed someone she could count on, someone she could trust, and he was neither. He hadn't even been able to bring himself to tell her exactly what had happened the night Daniel had died. All she knew was that *he*, Ben, been lauded like some kind of hero. Awarded a DSO—something which he certainly didn't deserve.

But he hadn't been able to bear to see either recrimination or pity in those dazzling sea-green eyes of hers. So instead he'd taken the coward's way out. Staying silent on the facts surrounding Daniel's death, and trying to make amends by fulfilling the promise he'd made to Dan. To provide her with a home, security and her education.

A gentle rapping on his door pulled him out of his reverie. Hauling the heavy wood open, he was surprised to see Thea in her coat and dressed to go out.

'Sorry, I didn't know if you were sleeping. I just wanted to let you know that I'm heading out, I've got a twenty-hour shift starting soon. I'm going in a bit early, and I won't be back until tomorrow afternoon.'

Twenty hours of focussed work to occupy the mind. That sounded really good right about now, Ben thought enviously. And he could understand her eagerness to leave the house early. This wasn't the easiest of arrangements.

'Sounds good.' He nodded. 'What is there to do around these parts these days? I might need something to do tomorrow.'

'Not a lot, to be honest' Thea pulled a face. 'Since you've gone all superhero maybe you could try the park. Or there's a little coffee house in the village up the road.'

Ben didn't answer. He'd deserved that. Instead he tried to smile and make it into a joke.

'So, what you really mean is, I have another day of nothingness to numb the brain.'

'Sorry.' She shrugged, moving quickly across the hallway to the stairs.

Feeling even more deflated, he exhaled heavily and closed the door again.

Tap-tap-tap.

'I thought you'd gone?' This time his smile was less forced as he opened the door. She was doing that lip-chewing thing again.

'Do you want to come with me?'

'To your work?'

By the look on her face, she was just as surprised he was by her offer. Still, she rallied well.

'Why not? I mean, I can see how you might be going a little mad with nothing to do. I think I would be too, in your position. And from a professional point of view I think you'd find it really interesting. The base is quite big and there are quite a few teams on site. Plus we've got a couple of ex-Army trauma specialists with us at the moment. You won't be able to come out on any calls, of course, but you can see how things go down at the base.'

'And today just happens to be *Take an Estranged Husband to Work Day*?' Ben grinned. The offer was tempting, but he couldn't see them letting him in.

'It might not be usual, but not *everyone* is the "Mighty Abs".' Thea deflected his scepticism with aplomb. 'A decorated major and renowned Army field trauma surgeon? Oh, I think they'll make an exception.'

Ben suppressed a shudder. 'Thanks for that.'

Still, if it meant getting out of this place and having something decent to distract him he wasn't about to grumble too loudly.

He grabbed his bomber jacket and followed her into the hallway. 'Lead the way.'

Thea made for the live feed screen on the wall the minute she stepped through the doors. Returning calls of greeting absentmindedly, she scrutinised the screen. It streamed real-time information on all incoming 999 calls for potential call-ups. Already she knew it had the potential to be a pretty busy day, but for now she had enough time to show Ben around.

Ben! She spun around with a start, but he'd already been whisked away. *Dammit.* Coming to work had provided the mental distraction she'd been craving, but it had also made her forget the one thing she needed to warn Ben about. That nobody actually knew she was married.

She felt physically nauseous as she dashed through the base, pulling up short as she spotted Ben in the break room, already surrounded by her colleagues. Well, she'd been right to suspect that he'd be more than welcome here, judging by the way everyone was falling over themselves to be introduced to him.

In one way it was a good sign—it meant she could give him the basic tour and then let someone else take over. Inviting him to join her certainly hadn't been an altruistic gesture. Being around Ben was proving even harder than she'd feared. Her little cottage, her haven, was now thick with tension, memories and unanswered questions. All of which she'd thought she had laid to rest a long time ago.

Seemed she'd been wrong.

So she'd brought Ben here. Hoping to prove to him just how much she'd changed in the last five years and perhaps hoping that their mutual love of medicine might offer them some interesting cases which they could discuss back at home—instead of strained one-liners as they skirted awkwardly around each other.

Caught up in anxious thoughts, she suddenly realised that everyone at the base had gone deathly silent. Apprehension gripped her as nine pairs of eyes fixed accusingly on her.

'Ben is your *husband*?'

'You're *married*?'

Dammit, she should have warned Ben to keep his mouth shut.

'Got a family tucked away we don't know about, too, Thea?'

That last quip had Thea's heart plummeting to the soles of her rubber rescue boots. They wouldn't be so quick to smile at her if they knew the truth. *Ben* wouldn't be so keen to be around her if *he* knew the truth.

'I... We... I...'

Of all the eyes boring into her it was the pair of familiar battleship-grey eyes she was most conscious of. *Ben's*. The pair she was keenest to avoid meeting.

Confusingly, she sensed the greatest level of accusation coming from him…and something else she couldn't quite pinpoint… *Could it be…hurt?* He had a damned nerve, she tried to tell herself.

'It's called a personal life for a reason, guys.' She tried to joke, but even to her ears it came across as prickly and standoffish.

'What my wife is trying to say is that it isn't easy being married to a soldier.' Ben stepped in, somehow managing to unruffle feathers and smooth things over with apparent ease. 'I've been on a lot of back-to-back tours and that's always…difficult.'

A series of grunts and nods told Thea they were buying it, and it was all she could do to stop her mouth from dropping open. Aside from the fact that it wasn't remotely close to the truth, why the heck couldn't Ben be so apparently open and communicative when it came down to what was *really* the problem between them?

As her colleagues drifted back to work, affording Ben and Thea a degree of space, Thea marvelled at their acceptance. If had been up to her, she wouldn't have lived it down for at least the next year.

She supposed she should be grateful to him. But she wasn't. She couldn't help noticing the way he'd fitted so seamlessly into her life, as though none of the pain of the last five years meant anything. She was beginning to wish she had never brought him here.

'So, what's next on the tour, Boss?' Ben asked pointedly, as if sensing her resentment and trying to push past it.

She opened her mouth before spotting one figure, leaning on a brick pillar, watching them. *Nic*, she realised with a start. She'd forgotten all about him. But even as she turned towards him he ducked his head and moved away.

'Who was that?' Ben asked quietly, moving to her shoulder.

She hesitated. Perhaps it was her resentment, or maybe guilt, but Thea found herself almost challenging Ben with her tone.

'That was Nic, another trauma doctor. We once dated.'

The shock in Ben's eyes was almost gratifying.

'What did you expect, Ben? That I'd been sitting around for five years, waiting for you?'

It felt good, almost cathartic, to say the words. He'd married her, given her one precious night and then walked out on her. For five years there had been no contact, and even now she was only with him for closure. It was galling that he had dropped back into her life with such apparent ease, as if he'd never been away. This was her way of reminding Ben that her life *hadn't* just stood still whilst she'd waited for him to return.

'No,' Ben answered softly at length. 'Our marriage was one of convenience. A marriage on paper—nothing more. You had every right to date. I did too.'

The admission was unceremoniously delivered, yet ridiculously it felt like a body blow. Unwelcome tears pricked the corners of her eyes and Thea blinked them away in confusion. Why should she react this way? She didn't care.

'You've dated?' she choked out.

Ben shrugged. 'A couple of times. Not seriously—the Army always came first.'

Somehow that made her feel better. Part of her had secretly hoped Ben would return, but mostly she had been grieving for the baby she'd lost, and it had taken her years even to think about starting to move on with anyone else. Eventually she'd tentatively started dating again, but it had mostly been abysmal—until Nic. He had been kind, and understanding, and a good communicator.

After Ben—after the baby—Nic should have been everything she wanted, or needed. But even then the wounds had still felt too close to the surface and she hadn't been able to let Nic in. Like it or not, a relationship with him just hadn't been what she'd wanted. She was only grateful that Nic had been as private a person as her, and so there were no other colleagues to whom they had to explain themselves.

She searched Ben's face, looking for clues. Realising there was nothing more to be said, she forced herself to move on.

'We've got three helicopters across two regional bases,' she announced flatly. 'So, between everything, we're never more than a fifteen-minute flight to the nearest hospital.'

He whistled. 'That's pretty impressive,' he said, after only a beat of hesitation.

He looked around to take it all in. She felt another odd swell of pride as he turned back to her, more questions at the ready.

'So, what's your range?'

'About six thousand square miles.' Thea indicated the map on the wall, showing the area in question, grateful to have something concrete to focus on. 'Our helicopters can fly up to around two hundred miles per hour, and are fitted out with the most advanced lifesaving kit to give the patients their very best possible chance of survival.'

Great—now she sounded like one of the charity's donation request adverts.

'Is it usually single individuals, or do you get multiple casualties?' he asked thoughtfully.

'Both,' she confirmed. 'From a single jockey or a skateboarder to a multi-car pile-up. The most I've triaged in one go is nine. So...let me show you around the base.'

'Thea, we're up.' One of the paramedics hurried over. 'Motorbike accident—twelve miles out.'

With little more than a cursory farewell to Ben, Thea

switched her mind from the complications and questions which had been dogging her all afternoon, and focussed in on her team.

Pulling her gear on, she listened as the base's switchboard operator relayed the details as they were fed to him.

'Two casualties—one rider, one pillion. High-speed collision with a car at a junction. There are two road crews already on their way to the scene but we've been called to attend.'

'We'll stay patched in. Keep us informed, Jack,' Thea said as she headed onto the Tarmac with the two paramedics on her team.

Her pilot, Harry, was already good to go, and as she jumped into the helicopter she brought up the crash location on her onscreen map, talking it through with him. Ultimately it would be his job to choose the optimal landing site.

As the helicopter ate up the relatively short distance to the crash site she kept an eye out for a clear landing location and potential hazards. A pass over the accident itself was an opportunity to take in as much detail as possible from the air—once on the ground it would be all go.

'There's a grassy central reservation—looks like we'll be able to land there. Just keep an eye out for power lines and street lights,' the pilot reminded her team, as he did every flight. It was part of their ritual, and it made sure they had their eye on the ball.

Thea drew in a few deep breaths as the pilot prepared to land the craft. This was the worst part. They were so close, and her adrenalin was coursing, but they had to be calm, patient. The pilot was lining the helicopter up between the street lights, with everyone systematically checking their own side, the rear, and below. It was always felt so painfully slow compared to the rest of the flight.

With an exhalation of relief, Thea felt the helicopter

touch down and she and her team jumped out. The road ambulance paramedics were waving her over to one crash victim. Even as she approached she could tell it was bad. The man's leg was open to the bone, presumably from his skid across the Tarmac of the road. But it was his silence which concerned her the most. She could hear his pillion passenger screaming in pain, but this man, the rider, was showing minimal response.

She hastily called in to update Jack, back at base, then turned her attention to their patients.

She couldn't assume the pillion rider was all right without checking, so she carried out a quick triage to confirm her suspicions.

'Stable, good SATS, broken leg and primarily superficial cuts and bruises.' She patched in the information to Jack.

But the other man wasn't so fortunate, and she suspected there would be a risk of amputation without immediate treatment—which was why her crew had been called out.

'Main casualty has open fracture on his knee. Suspected abdominal injury. Left side of chest severely compromised and he's in and out of consciousness. His SATS are down in the low eighties and I'm not happy that they won't drop out. I'm recommending ground ambulance, given the turbulence we experienced on the flight down and the short distance to the closest hospital. I'm going in the road ambulance—my guys too.'

If his SATS dropped again, or there were any other warning signs, Thea knew she would be able to spot them quickly and treat them. The fact that she was a trauma doctor was an advantage the air ambulance had over their road crew counterparts.

'You're clear for that.' Jack's voice responded immediately. 'Team Two are still on standby. I'll contact you if there are any emergencies.'

Giving her pilot a thumbs-up, telling him to return to the

helicopter and follow the team to the hospital, Thea swung herself up into the ambulance with the critically injured rider and began to work.

Ben watched as Thea jumped smoothly out of the helicopter, striding out across the Tarmac back to the base. It was her third call-out in twelve hours. She looked exhausted. And beautiful, Ben realised in a tumble of emotions. Emotions he had no place feeling, which were now vying for his attention. He fought to hold them back. He'd been emotionally prepared for the old Thea. But this Thea—this strong woman who seemed to bulldoze through all his carefully laid plans—was a different prospect.

As she walked into the base and her eyes collided with his, however, he could have sworn he saw her face fall.

'You were listening in the whole time?'

Why did he get the impression that whatever answer he gave it would be wrong?

'It was an interesting case.' He shrugged.

'But you would have done things better?'

Ben frowned, confused. From all he'd heard, her last patient had been DOA. No one could have done anything about that. But he stayed quiet, giving Thea a moment.

Did she think he was going to challenge her? Nothing could be further from the truth. Thea was good. She was more than good. She had to know that. This sudden hostility didn't seem to fit with the Thea he knew.

But how well do you really know her?

Ben tried to ignore the niggling reminder that she had never mentioned their marriage, even to her close-knit crew. He told himself it was hardly surprising, given that their marriage had been a sham anyway. But still, he felt oddly hurt and sidelined. She was getting under his skin again.

'It was another motorbike rider in a high-speed collision—this time with a truck in the oncoming lane.' Thea pushed past him into the break room, making her announcement to no one in particular and flinging her helmet down in frustration. 'She was pushed into the central reservation when someone pulled into the fast lane to overtake and didn't see the bike coming up behind. She clipped the barrier and flipped over into the oncoming traffic. DOA.'

'I'm sorry,' he sympathised.

'Why don't these people realise what happens to the human body when you come off one of those things?'

'One in three are dead on arrival.' One of the other paramedics looked up at Ben from his newspaper. 'Thea takes it personally. She wants to at least feel she stands a *chance* of helping the victims she's flown out to see.'

Ben nodded. He could understand that—it was something he had felt himself many times in the past. Perhaps it was conceit to think that he *could* have done something if the casualty had been alive when he arrived, rather than accepting that they were so badly injured they would have died whether or not he'd been there.

Still, he could empathise with Thea's frustration. And it was a relief to find common ground. It was as though it helped him to understand the woman Thea was now. As though it somehow brought them closer together.

He let his gaze fall back on Thea. She'd looked so calm and poised, hour after hour, call-out after call-out. Now, suddenly, she looked sad and deflated. He wanted to comfort her but she wouldn't welcome him. And besides, she didn't need him. She probably never had.

Still, wordlessly he moved into the kitchen to make her some strong, sweet tea.

He'd listened to her interactions with Jack every time her team had gone out, had admired her professionalism, her composure, her confidence. She commanded her team with respect and she knew how to get just that little bit more out of them—and her colleagues returned double that respect. Thea had seriously downplayed her talent when she'd told him she was good at her job. He'd be happy to have her work alongside him any time. No, scratch that, he'd be happy to work alongside *her* any time.

He felt a swell of pride which he had no right to feel. It was as though *he'd* had something to do with her success, and he knew that wasn't the case. She'd achieved this all on her own.

Still, this grown-up Thea was a far cry from the twenty-one-year-old Thea who had captivated him with her flightiness and her lust for life, combined with the gentle, almost shy side she'd kept hidden. This Thea was confident, ballsy and sexy, but utterly dedicated and focused on what really mattered. And, from the various admiring glances he'd seen cast her way, he wasn't the only one to think so.

He briefly wondered what had happened between Thea and Nic, before pushing the question aside. Who she dated wasn't his business. But the fact that she wanted to *was.* She was right about the Army not letting her stay in the house if they knew they weren't really married. But at some point she was bound to find someone else she *would* want in her life. And she and Ben needed an exit strategy.

He clenched his fists. The very thought simultaneously sickened and angered him. *Jealousy?* What was he playing at? This had to stop. *Now.*

Because he was beginning to think that he'd never be able to let her go. Not really. He didn't think he could stay in that house with her for longer than was absolutely necessary. The sooner he finished his recovery and got back to Army life, away from Thea, the better.

And not just Thea. He was feeling inexplicably drawn to the life she led here. Once, back-to-back tours had made him feel proud—as if he was achieving something. But more and more over the years he'd begun to feel disillusioned. As though he was fighting the same war over and over again but never getting anywhere. As though he'd be more effective elsewhere. Somewhere like here.

But he couldn't come here. This wasn't his life—it was hers. A life which she'd carved out for herself despite him. And he had no business being in it.

As much as he suddenly found himself wanting to.

CHAPTER FIVE

THEA RETREATED TO her bedroom the moment they returned to the cottage. It was the only sanctuary she had left now Ben had catapulted back into her life. She flopped onto her bed, expecting exhaustion to claim her, as it always did after a twenty-hour shift. But today it proved elusive and instead she twisted and turned in agitation.

Ben! she thought resentfully. She could hear him moving about in his own room, and even that riled her. She should have known when Ben had agreed to be discharged into her care that he would fight any real attempt to help him through his recovery. She'd been nothing more than a means to an end—a way for him to get away from the hospital and away from people. Because heaven forbid anyone should ever get close to him.

The only person Ben had ever appeared close to had been her brother Dan. Best mates and Army buddies, they would have laid down their lives for each other. Dan had done so. No wonder she could never compete with that in Ben's eyes.

She *harrumphed* and jettisoned herself off her bed to go and stare, unseeing, out of the window, lost in her thoughts.

What on earth had possessed her to invite Ben to work, to meet her colleagues, when she'd *known* it was bound to come out that she'd never told them she was married? Had she subconsciously *wanted* to create a confrontation? Neither of them had been prepared to be the first one to bring up their past, but now it was out there and she and Ben could no longer pretend to tiptoe around each other.

If it had been her unwitting intention, then it hadn't worked anyway. Ben didn't seem to care—not even about Nic. She didn't like to admit how much that hurt, but it *had* underlined things for her. She didn't want to keep avoiding their past—not when she still needed answers that only Ben could provide. They needed to have a conversation, at least once, which included the reason why he had *really* married her? The last time she'd asked him that he'd told her it had been the only way he could honour his promise to take care of her. But if that had been all there was to it then he wouldn't have slept with her.

She needed to understand. How could he have walked out on her that night?

And she wasn't the only one who was owed the truth. At some point she was going to have to tell him that she'd fallen pregnant that night and that she'd lost their baby. *But what if he didn't care?*

Thea turned around from the window. She was suffocating, trapped within the four walls of her room. She needed to get out of there.

She lunged across the room to the high chest of drawers and scrabbled for her running kit, but even now, as if taunting her, her eyes slid down to the bottom drawer. In there, tucked in a small brown envelope and slid out of sight under the maternity clothes she had bought in such excitement but which she'd never had opportunity to wear, was the scan image she had of the baby she'd lost.

She froze momentarily before wrenching her eyes away, focussing instead on the drawer crammed with sports gear. She needed to occupy herself, push herself to her limits, exhaust her body so that she might finally find the blissful oblivion of sleep.

Thea dressed within minutes and then ducked down the stairs and outside. She would stretch in the garden—it was a pleasant enough afternoon. A wave of relief flooded over her at her sense of freedom. But it was short-lived.

'Ben? You can't *seriously* be going out for a run?'

Instantly his expression of cautious greeting evaporated, closing down as he shut her out.

He sighed, as if humouring a small child. 'Look, I've jogged before—at the hospital.'

'Of *course* you have.' She snorted. *Why couldn't he just cut himself some slack?*

'Short distances, slow pace. I'll probably just jog down to the end of the road and back. How about you? How far are you going?

She bit her lip angrily. He was being foolish, but there was no way she was going to be able to talk him out of it. He was so stubborn.

'I was thinking five or six miles.' Thea stalled for a moment, contemplating cutting her stretches short. Ben couldn't afford to do anything to interfere with his body's healing process, but maybe she should jog away—stretch somewhere else.

Instead she stayed where she was, bending one leg up behind her, tucking her heel against her bottom to stretch her thigh. Refusing to be chased away.

Out of the corner of her eye she watched him move towards the gate. He was clearly pushing past his limits, against all medical advice. Suddenly she felt tired of telling him, tired of trying to be there for someone who clearly didn't want her help. So much for her hope that caring for Ben during his recovery would help her find the closure that she was so desperately lacking.

She took her time finishing her stretches, wanting to give Ben plenty of time to put some distance between them as he so clearly wanted to. She headed out in the opposite direction when she finally set off.

She wished it didn't matter. Over the years she'd almost convinced herself that she'd put Ben Abrams into her past. And then she'd received the news that he'd been blown up and was being shipped home. Her whole world had been thrown into chaos and she'd realised she'd never moved on from him, or from their wedding night, at all.

She'd been so silly in the beginning—racing home every day and hoping against hope that he'd be there, waiting for her. When she'd found out she was pregnant she'd believed that somehow he would sense it and come home. He hadn't. Just as he hadn't sensed it when she'd seen those first ominous spots of blood, or when the pain had hit, or when she'd lost their baby.

The loss had been visceral. And it had taken her so long to piece herself back together. How many times had she dialled the first few digits of Ben's mobile—wanting his strength, his comfort—only to terminate the call? She had needed him to come home because *he* had chosen to—not because she had compelled him. It had only been then that Thea had realised, deep down, that Ben was never coming back. She was on her own and she was always going to be on her own.

In the end she'd thrown herself into the last year of her degree, grateful for the long hours of exhausting work which had kept her out of the house and distracted her. A year to the day after she'd lost the baby Thea had finally picked up her first paintbrush and started the transitioning process, doing little bits of decorating on her few days off or when she'd found herself at a loose end.

Redecorating the house from top to bottom had been the only way she'd been able to occupy her thoughts and move on from what she had lost with Ben. It was no coincidence that her first—awful—date had taken place shortly after there had been no more decorating to do. Apart from Ben's room, which had remained untouched until last year.

If she looked back she wondered how she had managed to get through those dark, bleak days. So she'd stopped looking back, shut the memories away and pretended they belonged to someone else. And now she wasn't sure how to unlock them properly again, or even if she wanted to.

What purpose would it serve to tell Ben about the baby after all this time? And yet somehow she felt as though he had a right to know.

It piqued her to realise that, deep down, she *wanted* to tell him. But she still couldn't shake the fear that he might not care.

Thea stopped running, her legs suddenly sapped of strength. She shook her head, but her doubts weren't so easily dislodged. Nor was her darkest and yet most precious secret.

Caught up in her thoughts, she didn't realise she had run for miles in a long circuit, eventually coming to the park where Daniel had used to train. Suddenly she found herself in front of the long, steep hill on which, as a kid, she had sometimes watched him complete hill rep after hill rep before they talked about life, school, and whether anyone was bullying her. Inexorably drawn there, Thea wished she had her brother to talk to now. But then if Daniel had still been alive she wouldn't have been in this predicament with Ben in the first place.

Unexpectedly she felt her eyes prick with tears and took a step backwards, struggling for breath. Five years and she had pretty much come to terms with losing her brother. These days it rarely caught her off guard like that.

She suspected that her earlier thoughts of Ben had a lot to do with her scattered emotions. No matter what she did, she couldn't seem to get away from him.

Thea jerked her head up as sudden movement over the dip caught her eye. As if to prove her point, Ben came gradually into view, evidently pushing through every pain barrier. He saw her and, even from that distance the clenching of his jaw betrayed the little muscle ticing in irritation.

'Daniel used to train here.' She wrapped her arms defensively across her chest as he approached.

'Hill reps—yes. I know.'

'You trained here together?' Realisation dawned. 'Daniel brought me here sometimes, to talk and to jog around the lake with him.'

'I never thought… Of course. You miss him,' Ben stated flatly. 'I'm sorry. I didn't mean to intrude on your memories. I'll leave you to your peace. See you back at the house, Thea.'

Abruptly Thea wondered if, like her, Ben's memories were what had drawn him here today. To her, Ben's accident sounded similar to what had happened to Daniel. Certainly the ambush and getting pinned down by the enemy. She wondered if Ben was feeling as disconcerted about their being back at cottage together as she was. She wasn't sure why that made her feel a little better, but it did. It offered her a new sense of courage.

'No—wait.' Quickly she put a hand out to touch Ben's arm, to stay him, but she wasn't prepared for the jolt that fizzed through her.

Snatching her fingers swiftly away, she forced herself to meet his eyes. *That wasn't supposed to happen.* It certainly wasn't what she *wanted* to happen.

Still, it was proving impossible for them to live together. As much as they had tried to ignore the problem, accusations hung silently around them every time they walked into the same room. She'd been right earlier. Pretending the issues between them didn't matter wasn't working. At some point they *would* have to talk. And now, here, seemed as good a time as any.

'Don't leave. We both came here for a reason.'

'This isn't the time.' Ben turned, ready to move away.

I think this *is* the time,' Thea argued. 'Don't *you* have questions? Because I have.'

So many.

'I know what your questions are, Thea.' He turned slowly back, meeting her gaze head-on. 'But I can't give you the answers you want to hear.'

'You don't know what I want to hear.'

'I think I do.'

It was like some surreal stand-off, neither of them wanting to blink first.

Across the lake a little girl threw oats onto the water. Ducks fought for them and other birds tweeted as they flew gracefully in from overhead. The little girl laughed and turned to her mother for more. She was four, maybe five. Briefly Thea wondered if that might have been her and their child, if things had been different. It all seemed so familial and idyllic—a stark contrast to the turmoil going on in her head and the thunderous pounding in her chest. It made her stand her ground all the more.

As if sensing the subtle change, Ben conceded. 'All right—what do you want to know, Thea?

It wasn't exactly encouraging a proper dialogue between them, but it was better than him shooting her down as he had in the past.

She sucked in a deep breath. 'Why did you marry me, Ben?'

The words seemed to hang in the stillness of the park. Ben stopped shifting but didn't immediately turn to face her. By the look on his face and the steel-shuttered set of his eyes it seemed his acquiescence of a moment ago had merely been his attempt to humour her.

'You asked me what I wanted to know,' she prompted urgently. 'This is it.'

'We've been through this. It was the only way to take care of you properly in a way the Army would accept.'

'Yes, but then you slept with me. And ever since I've wondered if there was something more to your offer.'

'I'm sorrier than you can ever imagine for that night.' Ben gritted his teeth, disgust etched onto his features.

'*Are* you?' Thea asked desperately. 'Only I think maybe you wanted me as much as I wanted you.'

His Adam's apple bobbed but he said nothing for several long moments. 'Of course I wanted you,' he ground out at length.

'Is that why you married me? Because even though you told me we weren't a good match you still…obviously you didn't love me, but *lusted* after me?' She flushed red, embarrassed by the words.

'I married you because Dan asked me to look after you and it was the only way to get Army approval,' Ben repeated flatly. 'He asked me to take care of you. He was my best friend. I agreed.

'As simple as that?' she snapped in frustration. 'Really?'

But Ben didn't bite back. 'As simple as that.'

She swallowed down the sarcastic retort on her lips. What was it about Ben that had her feeling like a desperate twenty-one-year-old again? She was a successful, respected trauma doctor, so why, after five years, was it still so important to her to know if something more than just a casual promise to her brother had driven Ben to marry her? Something more emotional. The same something which had sparked between them when they'd slept together, perhaps?

Surely it hadn't just been her imagination.

Judging by the way he shifted edgily, she was getting under his skin as much as he was getting under hers right now. Somehow it offered her some small comfort.

'For heaven's sake Thea.' He tugged his hand through his hair irascibly. 'What does this conversation gain for us? How we felt or didn't feel—it doesn't change anything.'

'It does for me,' Thea half-whispered. 'It matters to *me*.'

'Why? Why does it matter *now*?'

She faltered, licked her lips nervously. 'Because in all these years you've never really told me what happened between you walking me home and saying how *connected* we were on that first date and then, almost within hours, telling me you weren't interested.' She had never been able to help wondering if she'd done something wrong.

The seconds ticked by between them and she was sure he must be able to hear her heart beating out of her chest.

'Okay, I liked you,' Ben shrugged, as if it was no big deal. As if *she* was no big deal. 'But then I walked you up that driveway and Dan came to the door, bellowing his head off. The minute I realised you were his sister you were off limits, Thea. We'd just met, had one simple date—what did it matter?'

Thea shook her head. 'It wasn't just a *simple date*, though.'

Not for her—and, according to Ben, not for him either. He had been the first person she'd met who had seen through her bubbly façade to the uncertain, slightly bruised person underneath. Her brother had done an incredible job of making her feel loved, a secure and rounded person—but nothing had ever made up for losing her parents as a kid. Nothing had ever taken away the uncertainty that had brought. Not completely.

And Ben had seen that. She'd never met anyone with whom she'd clicked so perfectly—either before or since. To someone who had perfected the art of letting people *think* they were getting close to her, Ben had been the first and only person who had ever slipped past her defences—effortlessly—and *really* got to her.

Ben shrugged, again reaching for the easiest explanation. 'You were Dan's sister—'

'No,' she interrupted. She knew what was coming and she didn't want to hear it. 'Not that *"Buddy Code"* bull you and Daniel had about not dating each other's kid sister. Not this time. You won't trust each other with your sisters, but you'll trust each other with your life?'

'Out there we'll take a bullet for each other. It's not a game, Thea. It's war. Dating is the least of our problems. People *die* out there.'

His words were like a kick to the stomach. But she had lost too much to be fobbed off so easily.

'You think I don't *know* that soldiers die out there?' She gasped. 'You might have lost your best friend, Ben, but I lost my *brother*.'

He stared at her wordlessly for a moment, with a death-like pallor. He gave a sharp nod, as though acknowledging her point for the first time.

'Why don't you ever talk about him?' Thea asked suddenly.

He blanched, and it was like a door clicking open in her head. How was it that she'd observed Ben's avoidance in the past but never really *noticed* it?

Had she missed something fundamental all this time?

'Why don't you ever talk about *yourself*?'

'There's nothing to tell.'

He drew his lips into a thin line, refusing to be drawn by her. She couldn't remember ever seeing him look shaken or uncertain. If she really thought about it she could only picture the determined, closed-off, emotionless Ben of the past. A picture of him pieced together after their date, their few weeks together between Ben telling her about Daniel's death and the moment she and Ben married, and the many fragments of stories Daniel had told her about Ben.

Whatever had started this conversation, she felt the urge to push him that little bit harder before he had time to pull that impenetrable armour of his back into place. She might never get the chance again.

'Ben?'

'I *liked* you, Thea,' he suddenly blurted out. 'I liked you a lot. Maybe too much.'

'What does *"too much"* mean?' she asked instinctively, but Ben was already shaking his head, back-pedalling. Did it mean the Buddy Code was just an excuse—as she'd always wondered?

'It doesn't mean anything, 'Ben growled. 'Forget I said it. I just mean I thought you were incredible. But when I realised you were Dan's sister I knew we weren't a good match.'

'You didn't know anything about me.' She frowned.

He opened his mouth, as though he had something more to say, and then the shuttered look she knew so well came down over his face.

'You're right—we didn't know much about each other,' he conceded. 'But then I made a promise to take care of you, and that was what I intended to do.'

The moment was lost, Thea realised in despair. Whatever had made him drop his guard a few moments earlier, it was gone now.

'So because of that promise you ended up with a wife you'd never wanted? A bad match? No wonder you abandoned me.' Frustration tinged her words with bitterness.

'*Abandoned* you?'

Ben whipped his head around to stare at her, shock clouding his handsome features. Then it was gone, and the mask of indifference was back, leaving Thea wondering if she'd imagined it.

'When did I *abandon* you?'

'The morning after our wedding. The morning after...' She swallowed, suddenly nervous '...after *that* night.'

'I didn't abandon you. You told me to leave.'

'Sorry? I did *what*?' She was incredulous.

'I did what you asked me to do.' His voice was low, urgent. His eyes were raking desperately over her.

'That's ridiculous!' she cried.

He would *not* wriggle out of this. *But, God, it was humiliating.* She'd offered herself up to him that night, convinced that there had been more to his marriage proposal, that deep down he still liked her even if he couldn't admit it. Clearly her mistake, but if Ben had wanted to honour his promise to her brother surely he should have understood that she'd been grief-stricken and had made an enormous error of judgement? Not walked out on her, leaving her all alone.

'You left when I needed you most. I felt alone…deserted. I'd just buried my brother. I never thought *you'd* leave me like that.'

'You needed space.'

'I needed *support*!' she cried.

'You needed someone you trusted,' Ben countered. 'And after we slept together you didn't trust me. Why should you? I'd taken advantage of you when you were at your most vulnerable.'

'You didn't take advantage of me.' Thea shook her head.

'Of course I did,' Ben spat in self-contempt. 'You even told me that it was one of the most horrific days of your life,' he told her.

'You know it was,' Thea muttered. 'I'd just buried my brother, and yet I was getting married.'

Little wonder that her head had been a confused jumble of emotions. Even though time had passed, she still didn't like to dwell too long on the bitter memories.

'You told me that you'd thought us sleeping together would make it better,' Ben recalled. 'But that it had just made it worse.'

'Because I'd spent those six weeks between our date and the night we slept together hoping, deep down, that you would realise your mistake in ending things. I hoped you still had feelings for me and I thought our sleeping together would help you admit it. Instead you rejected me. *Again*. I felt more alone than ever.'

She watched the rise and fall of his chest as he absorbed what she was telling him, part of her hoping he'd tell her that it had all been just some big misunderstanding and they could have been with each other all this time if only they'd realised.

But that was nonsense, wasn't it? Because it hadn't been a misunderstanding. Ben was never going to talk to her, open up to her. There was some element of survivor's guilt too, which she couldn't afford to underestimate. But ulti-

mately Ben would *never* be able to open up to her, talk to
her about his emotions.

No misunderstanding could change that.

And what about *her*? She'd idolised Ben even before
she'd ever met him, having fallen in love with the incredible
war stories of him as brave hero which Daniel had told her
growing up. In her head Ben had already been extraordinary. So even if he *had* been able to talk to her and reveal
his weaknesses would she have actually listened? Would
she ever have allowed him the hopes, the fears, the disap-
pointments of any ordinary man?

Thea couldn't be sure. Unlike Ben, who hadn't known
her when they'd met that first night and gone on that first
date, *she* had known exactly who Ben was. So in some way
perhaps she'd brought this on herself.

Not that she could ever admit that to Ben. If he ever realised that she'd known who he was that first time they'd
met and not told him he would think she'd been manipula-
tive, that her actions had been deliberate. But they hadn't.
At worst she'd been naive, even foolish, but she had never
intended anyone to get hurt.

When she'd first seen him walk into that club with his
friends she'd been drawn to him, but she hadn't realised
why. Not at first. She'd watched him for a while, liking the
way he interacted with his group. He'd seemed as if was
having fun, but he hadn't been rowdy, like some of the guys
she'd known. She'd watched several girls approach him,
and although he'd been friendly enough he hadn't seemed
overly interested in any of them.

When he'd gone to the bar she'd taken her opportunity
and slipped through the crowd to join him. The ease with
which they'd struck up a conversation had seemed like
a sign. Even when she'd found out his name she hadn't
put two and two together, but as the evening had worn on
she'd found their instant attraction developing quickly into

something more—in one evening she had known she really liked him.

It had only been later that night—when he'd mentioned excusing himself from his Army buddies—that she'd asked him about his job and suddenly realised why he'd seemed so familiar to her, why she'd felt so instantly at ease in his company. She'd seen him before—in a rare photo Dan had from an early tour in Afghanistan.

Dan had told her so many stories about Ben as hero that when she'd seen him walk in—even though she might not have realised it—she'd already known he was a good guy. More than just a good guy. But she hadn't been able to bring herself to spoil the evening or have it come to an abrupt end by telling him she was Daniel's sister. She'd already liked him too much to risk him walking away before he had taken the time to get to know her.

Yes, she'd been foolish and naive, caught up in the myth of 'Ben the Hero', but she hadn't deliberately set out to deceive anyone.

Putting Ben on a pedestal, idolising him—that had been no basis for a stable marriage. And if he hadn't walked out on her she might never have realised how truly strong she was, how much she could achieve. She might never have become the successful, respected doctor that she was today.

In some perverse way she should be grateful to him for abandoning her. For not loving her. It was a *good* thing. But it didn't feel like that.

She'd moved on a long time ago, so why did it feel as though a childhood dream, a girlish fantasy, had just died? That things were never going to be the same again? She had wanted to see Ben through his recovery in order to gain closure, but she'd never expected to gain it this way.

Well, she almost had closure—she still needed to tell him about the baby. *Their* baby.

But not today. Another day. When she was feeling stronger.

'I don't know what to say…' Ben began. 'I'm sorry.'

'There's nothing to say.'

Thea stood up abruptly. Her humiliation was almost complete and she'd brought it all on herself. She'd laid her heart out there for him and he still wasn't able to tell her he'd really wanted her.

'I've got my answer. Thank you for being honest with me.'

'Thea, listen…'

She held up her hand to stop him.

'Please, Ben, don't say anything. You've answered my questions. It's not your fault if I don't like what I heard.'

Quickly she turned and jogged away, before the tears which were pooling in her eyes could begin to fall.

CHAPTER SIX

BEN SAT BOLT-UPRIGHT. The blood was gushing in his ears, his heart was hammering out of his chest, his body was drenched in sweat. Nightmares. *Again.*

He forced his head to focus on the clock. Two-thirty a.m.

Pushing himself out of bed, he tried to escape his unwanted thoughts. But not even standing under the hot, powerful jets of the shower, almost too exhausted to raise his arms, could wash away the doubts which had long since lurked in his subconscious but were now beginning to break the surface.

The events of yesterday had played through his head all night—events from the moment Thea had left him at the park.

He felt mentally and physically exhausted, and he knew it wasn't just from pushing his body too hard yesterday. Although he had. He'd pushed himself too hard from the moment he'd got out from under the hospital's watchful eye—he knew that. Thea had been right about him pushing past his limits. The pain was almost constant now, rather than easing off bit by bit, day by day, as it should be.

But he almost welcomed it.

It meant that he was still alive when so many others were dead—his men, his friends, Dan.

He must never slack off—never let the injuries defeat him. He felt ashamed that only a few months ago, when he'd first woken in that hospital, paralysed and groggy, he'd closed his eyes and prayed that when he went back to sleep he wouldn't wake up again.

He was so very grateful he *had* woken again. And now he owed it to the memory of every soldier who had died out there never to let himself fall that far again. He needed to get his body back to full health, pass his Army Medical Board and get back to whichever war zone they wanted to send him to, save as many lives as he could.

He also needed to get out of this house, before he did something he regretted. Like giving in to temptation with Thea the way he had on their wedding night.

And right now that was proving harder than ever.

Her revelations yesterday had been a bombshell. He still couldn't quite get his head around it. He'd spent five years believing that he'd betrayed Thea, taken advantage of her in her grief, and he had hated himself for it. He'd left the following morning because he had genuinely believed Thea had wanted him to. His shame had been the only thing which had stopped him from making contact in all these years. He had believed she must abhor him even more than he loathed himself. Instead Thea was now telling him that he hadn't taken advantage of her vulnerability at all—that she had actively *wanted* him on their wedding night. As much as he had wanted her.

And that raised a whole other problem.

Thea's frankness yesterday had caught him off guard. She had his emotions starting to spiral out of control, and for someone who had always been taught to put his feelings in a box and shut them neatly away it was all a completely alien experience.

Slamming the shower off, hearing the *clunk-clunk* of water hammering through the pipes, he hoped it wasn't reverberating around the silent house and waking Thea. Still, the noise aptly mirrored his sour mood. He half-heartedly patted his body down with a towel and then shuffled across to his bedroom to flop, exhausted, back into bed.

He didn't expect to sleep, but the psychological impact of Thea's revelation was taking its toll on his still healing body. As soon as his head had hit the pillow sleep engulfed him, and he slept for four hours straight.

By the time he awoke the blinding pain of yesterday had receded to a dull ache and he felt somewhat revived, a little less tense. He listened carefully. They were going to have to build some bridges, but right now he could do without bumping into Thea. Reassured that the house was silent, Ben climbed out of bed and crept quietly out of the room and down the stairs to the kitchen.

'For crying out loud!'

As Ben stepped through the door he ducked just in time to miss a high-flying empty juice carton which a clearly exasperated Thea had just over-armed towards the swing bin. It hit the sweet spot and tumbled in.

Time to start bridge-building after all.

'Nice shot.'

It might have been weak but it was a start, although her grunt of response wasn't encouraging. Neither was the fact that she'd flushed bright red and was refusing to meet his eye, sitting straighter, more rigid on her stool. No doubt she was feeling raw and embarrassed after their last conversation. And that was his fault too.

He cast around for something else to say and noticed the glass sitting forlornly on the countertop, next to where Thea was. There was barely a trickle in the bottom, but the same carton had been over half full when he'd taken it from the fridge last night. Hence the flying missile, he realised.

'Sorry about the juice,' he apologised. 'I meant to go out early this morning and pick another one up, but...'

She shot a sharp look his way and he realised she thought he was having a dig at her. His gut twisted. He'd had no idea he'd hurt her so badly; it certainly hadn't been his intention, and making amends was going to prove harder than anticipated if she was still smarting from their confrontation yesterday.

Now was his chance to say something. But the words

wouldn't come. Instead he told himself that Thea had finally got a long-held resentment off her chest and he couldn't blame her for any of it. Raking it all up again in the cold light of today wouldn't help anybody.

Thea might not realise it, but she had changed so much in the last five years from the young woman he remembered. She was successful, settled and happy, and just because she'd taken the opportunity to vent it didn't mean she wanted to be dragged into his emotional baggage. What was it she'd said? *There's nothing more to say.*

Caught up in his musings, he almost jumped when the toaster popped up a teacake. He gave a wry smile. He'd forgotten how much she loved them. Dan had once told him that teacakes were the reason she'd dragged him to endless teashops—one of the many things he'd affectionately recounted about his kid sister.

What was he doing, reminiscing? There was no place in this scenario for such sentimental nonsense. Thea needed something more tangible from him. A matter of a few weeks ago she'd asked for a semblance of friendship— well, now was his chance to try it.

He glanced at her. She was ignoring the teacake, still rigid on her stool. Reaching over, he took the teacake and placed it on the plate she'd set by the toaster, then slid it over to her with a smile.

'An olive branch?'

'Thanks,' she muttered. 'Um…could you please pass me the butter as well?'

'Sure.' Surprised, he obliged.

Thea slipped off her stool and appeared to shuffle to the cutlery drawer, careful to keep the counter in between them. It was only when he leaned over to slide the butter tray across the island that he understood her discomfort.

Just beyond the countertop he caught a glimpse of the curve of her pert backside, peeking out from beneath a short, cheeky dressing gown. Unexpectedly desire fired through him. He wondered what would happen if he rounded the island and took her in his arms. Claimed her mouth with his, reminding her of what she'd once wanted with him. What they had *both* once wanted.

'Ben?'

He snatched his gaze up to see her staring at him, her eyes wide, a horrified expression on her face as she tugged desperately at the dressing gown, dropping the knife in the process. It hit the floor with a loud clatter.

What was wrong with him?

Disgust flooded through him and he turned away, angry with himself for letting his lust take over when he was supposed to be focussed on making amends to Thea. He still wanted her, after all this time, but he had no right to.

Her flushed face turned an even deeper shade of scarlet and then she was scurrying around the island, head down and mumbling something. *Hell.* That was his fault. *Again.* He'd made her feel uncomfortable in her own home.

He stepped into her path to block her exit. 'Thea, I'm sorry. That shouldn't have happened.'

'I thought you were asleep when I came down...'

She paused for a moment, shaking her head, biting her lip. Then she stepped forward placing her hands flat on his chest as if to gently move him out of her way. Reaction fizzed through him, and by the way her head jerked up and she looked him in the face Thea felt it too.

They stood motionless for several moments, unable to break whatever spell momentarily bound them. Then he moved his hands to cover hers and took a step closer. She didn't back away. He could feel her breath, soft and warm on the back of his hand. He wondered if she could feel his heartbeat accelerating beneath her touch. It was practically hammering its way right out of his chest, and the desire to kiss her was overwhelming.

Ben dipped his head, then paused.

He wasn't sure who pulled away first, but in an instant

they were stumbling awkwardly away from each other, snatching their hands back as if they'd been burned and muttering incoherently.

And then she was gone and Ben stood alone, fumbling to regroup. He glanced around the kitchen, wondering what had just happened between them.

'You're early,' Jack noted as soon as Thea walked onto the base for her shift. 'Your shift doesn't start for an hour. What's up? Trouble in paradise?'

'What?' Thea looked at him sharply.

'Difficult to get used to being around each other again?' Jack shrugged. 'When a soldier comes back to civilian life after a long time away at war? The readjustment period, isn't it?'

'Oh. Right. Yes.' Thea forced herself to smile.

If only it was that. She had no idea what had happened between them this morning. Except that she'd let her emotions—her desire for Ben Abrams—get to her again. She knew better than that—at least her head did. So why couldn't her heart toe the line as well? There could be no future for them—especially after she'd laid everything out to him, spilled her heart, and all he'd been able to say was an unsatisfactory *sorry.*

She wondered if deep down she'd been holding out for some declaration of love—if only to restore some of her bruised sense of pride. She didn't *want* a romantic relationship with Ben—they had too much painful history and logically she knew it would never work out between them. But clearly he'd never once regretted his decision to leave, never once thought about her or wondered what might have been. And that hurt more than she would have thought possible after all this time.

She ought to be resolved to it. But she'd woken up this morning wondering if maybe they *could* salvage something out of this mess, if she *could* set aside her wounded pride. The beginnings of a tentative friendship, perhaps?

Instead she'd made another spectacle of herself.

Even now her cheeks burned when she thought of what she'd been wearing when he'd walked in. She'd thought he would sleep longer. Through the wall she'd heard his bad night, so she hadn't expected him to come down to the kitchen until she'd left, but he hadn't known that.

She could recall the look of pure disgust on his face with humiliating clarity. He was going to think she was throwing herself at him all over again—especially after wearing her heart on her sleeve yesterday. And then, as if hell-bent on making matters worse, she'd hung on to him like a limpet when *he'd* been politely trying to lift her hands from his chest, unable to shake off the deep, longing desire which had flooded her body as soon as the two of them had come into contact.

'Thea? Did you hear what I said?'

'Hmm? Oh, sorry...' She cast Jack an apologetic look.

'I thought not.' He sighed, then warned her, 'I was telling you to watch out—Sir James has been after you.'

'Sir James? What does *he* want?' She could do without any added stress today. The man never called in without a reason, and it wasn't usually good.

'Not here—on the phone,' Jack reassured her. 'You probably need to call him sooner rather than later. The office should be free.'

'You're probably right.' Thea pulled a face as she trudged to the door. 'The last thing anyone wants is to be caught in Sir James's sights if he comes down here to reprimand me in person.'

'Thea?' Are you okay? You look white as a sheet.'

Thea was startled when Nic walked into the office. How long had she sat staring at the phone after her call to Sir

James had ended? She stared bleakly up into Nic's concerned face.

'What's wrong, Thea?'

'That was Sir James.' Her voice sounded hollow. 'About Ben.' She stopped, shooting Nic an apologetic look. 'I'm sorry. You're probably the last person who wants to hear about Ben.'

'You mean the husband I never knew you had?' Nic answered wryly. 'And the fact that I dated his wife—presumably you *were* married when we dated?'

'God, I'm so sorry. I should have told you. I just never... I shouldn't have...'

'Thea.' Nic pulled her hands gently away from her face. 'It's okay.'

'Is it? How can you be fine about it?' Thea asked incredulously. 'I mean, I'm grateful that you are, but I feel like I lied to you.'

'No, you didn't.' Nic pulled a wry face. 'Don't you remember turning me down twice before finally giving in to my charms? And even then you warned me that it was just a taster date between friends.'

'I remember.' Thea blinked. *How had she forgotten that before?*

'I always suspected that there was someone else—or at least that there had been someone.'

Thea was silent. She couldn't tell Nic that it hadn't been because she'd still been in love with Ben, more that the wounds had still been too close to the surface. Especially the miscarriage.

'So...' Nic gently broke into her thoughts. 'What did Sir James say to upset you?'

'They want Ben to work here.'

'Ah.'

'You don't sound surprised.'

'Honestly? I'm not. You know how tight-knit our medical community is. I'd heard about Major Ben Abrams even before you rolled up here and shocked us all with the revelation that he's your husband. He's one of the most pioneering trauma surgeons in today's war zones. Some of his techniques have already filtered down to the likes of you and I. Plus…' Nic grinned again. 'He's the hero who miraculously survived *two* IEDs and is back up and walking in almost half the time of any most other patients.'

'Jogging, actually.' Thea arched her eyebrows at him, still trying to calm her racing thoughts.

'You're kidding?' He stared at her, as if waiting for the punchline. 'You're not kidding. The man must be a machine.'

The man has demons, she thought. Ben pushed himself and pushed himself, and even now she didn't fully understand his reckless drive. If he didn't confront his fears soon then he was likely going to self-destruct.

And if he was here, working with her every day, wasn't there a chance she would let herself be dragged down with him?

She dropped her head into her hands. How was she supposed to work alongside the man?

'Okay,' Nic continued eventually, 'tell me what Sir James said.'

Thea drew in a deep, steadying breath, trying to still her spinning head.

'He said what you've just said—about Ben being a cutting-edge trauma surgeon, skilled in field techniques which will really benefit us on Civvy Street. He reminded me that the Air Ambulance is a charity, and that someone like Ben could really help to raise our profile and secure us extra funding. And he informed me that there are many other interested parties trying to court Ben in the event that he doesn't return to active duty.'

'So far, so Sir James,' Nic muttered. 'But surely the idea of Ben not returning to active duty appeals to you?'

Thea snorted. 'Ben would *never* give up an opportunity to return to full Army life.'

'He might. For you.'

She opened and closed her mouth a few times.

'That's lunacy. And anyway... I'd never ask him to do that.'

'I didn't say you would. So, let me guess. Sir James threatened your place here if you don't talk to Ben.'

'Not in so many words. But he implied that he would have to think twice about someone who didn't have the best interests of the charity at the forefront of her mind,' Thea agreed.

'Why doesn't that surprise me? Okay. Forget Sir James and his threats—look at it another way. If it was anyone other than Ben, would you be in favour of it?'

'I... Well...' Thea blinked at him, for the first time really stopping to think.

'For what it's worth...' Nic spoke again '... I have to admit I wouldn't mind learning from a trauma guy of Ben's calibre. Imagine the potential to save lives we might otherwise lose.'

'That's what Sir James said. *"Imagine if the Major's knowledge could help you save just one additional life you might otherwise have lost."*'

'The old guy's devious, but he has a point,' Nic conceded. 'Even one precious life.'

Thea felt a shiver creep over her back. *One precious life.* She knew the value of that. She was a trauma doctor. But just for a moment she'd been ready to become a mother. What wouldn't she give to have a happy four-year-old running around now?

Her heart flip-flopped. She had no choice. Somehow she was going to have to try and forge a friendship with

Ben. Until she did they wouldn't possibly be able to work in the tense atmosphere which surrounded them when they were together.

'You're right. I'll speak to Ben tomorrow.'

CHAPTER SEVEN

It was just after midday when Ben heard Thea moving in her room. She'd got in from her shift at six a.m. and had crashed out for the last few hours. He waited impatiently for her to shower and head downstairs. If they were going to make this arrangement work then it was time to re-establish some basic ground rules—especially since that unexpected moment between them in the kitchen yesterday morning.

However much he wanted to deny it, there was still some spark between them, and they needed to address that. They couldn't afford for it to happen again.

Thea had moved on with her life without him there to complicate things and was now a successful trauma doctor. And in a few months he would be returning to his Army life, able to bury his feelings for Thea once again.

'I want to apologise for all the drama since I came home,' he announced, once she'd come down and they'd dispensed with the small-talk. 'I can imagine it hasn't been easy having me here, bursting back into your life and disrupting your routines. So I'd like us to try and start over.'

'Start over? How?'

He could hear the caution in her tone and forced himself to smile brightly. 'Try to forge some kind of a friendship. Like you suggested.'

She licked her lips and a fresh wave of lust coursed through him. *Get a grip,* he chastised himself, but the image of those long, slender legs of hers, and that perfect backside, popped into his head.

This was exactly why he needed to confront things. Put a stop to this unwelcome lust now.

'I've made you some breakfast, by the way. Plus I bought you two fresh cartons of cranberry juice. Can I get you a glass?'

She looked around the room, her eyes scanning everything, her nose sniffing appreciatively and her stomach offering a low grumble despite her reservations.

'Well, it's not cereal,' she quipped, clearly attempting to meet him halfway.

He couldn't help being surprised—and pleased. He hadn't thought it would be so easy to convince her.

'Pancakes,' he confirmed, gesturing to the array of syrups, jams and fruit he'd bought. 'Listen, Thea, I need you to know how sorry I am. This is all new to me. I know how to be a good field surgeon, I know how to be a good commander, and I know how to be a good soldier. But I don't know how to do *this...*'

'Normality?' Thea suggested when he floundered.

'Domesticity,' Ben confirmed. 'I'm out of my comfort zone. I'm sorry if this seems corny to you, but this is me trying to make amends.'

'So you made pancakes?' She raised her eyebrows, sliding in at the breakfast bar and watching him slide a fluffy disc from the pan onto a plate. 'I didn't even know you could cook.'

'I like to eat—the two go together. Besides, pancakes aren't really cooking.' He shrugged, grateful for her acceptance. 'But they're my Achilles' heel—especially with maple syrup, a handful of berries and dollop of cream. They're why I have to train so much—just so that I can keep eating.'

He tapped his chest, as if to prove his point, and saw Thea let her gaze drop over his body. She snatched her eyes away, two spots of colour flushing her creamy, smooth cheeks.

She was still attracted to him despite what she'd said last night, he realised abruptly.

His reaction was instantaneous and he shifted uncomfortably. *This* was what he had to avoid. He'd allowed his desire for her to drive his actions once before, and he'd ended up having to walk away from her, having to—what had she said?—*abandon her*. And nothing had changed. He still couldn't give Thea what she needed, provide emotional support the way she wanted. He was still broken—perhaps now more than ever. He could never be the man Thea deserved.

He was stalling. If he didn't speak now would he allow himself to back out?

'I owe you an apology,' he said quickly. 'The things you said at the park the other day...'

'Oh, Ben, please don't...' She backed up immediately, waving her hand around as if she was trying to swat a fly. 'Could we just pretend all that never happened—?'

'No.' He interrupted her embarrassed stuttering firmly. 'You were honest and open yesterday, but I wasn't. I'm sorry.'

She narrowed her gaze uncertainly at him, her voice tentative. 'What weren't you honest about?'

'You asked me what I meant by liking you *too much*, and if the Buddy Code was just an excuse. I didn't give you a straight answer.'

'No, you didn't,' she said nervously.

'I think maybe it *was* an excuse.'

Simple. Direct.

He would have needed a serrated knife to cut the tension. He hated this kind of conversation, talking about his feelings, but if they were going to get past their baggage he needed to make himself do this. Just this once.

'I should have told you that the night I first met you— that one spontaneous date—you made me feel the most alive and yet the most relaxed I've ever felt outside of a field hospital.'

'Coming from you, that's quite a compliment,' Thea murmured, pouring herself some juice.

'It might not sound like it, but it is,' Ben told her. 'That was the only place I'd ever felt comfortable. As though I belonged and was happy. Until I met you. You had me telling you things I'd never told anyone before…about my childhood…my mother…'

'You miss her,' Thea said simply.

Ben felt his jaw lock. He never said the words—even in his head. It was difficult even hearing someone else say them. Still, he forced himself to nod.

'Yes. But we never talk about her—my father and I. We don't do this…*touchy-feely* stuff.'

He pulled a face. This incredible woman had lost both her loving parents at such a young age, and yet she still believed in love. How could he explain to her that the relationship between *his* parents had been so different? Even before her death his father's too-serious nature had stifled his mother's vibrant spirit. After she had died the last fragile threads of the relationship between Ben and his father had been irreparably ruptured.

What if Ben damaged relationships the same way? After all, it was all he'd ever known.

He wrenched his head from his black thoughts and back to Thea.

'When you and I had that one date together you completely blindsided me.'

'How?'

He'd had a feeling she was going to ask that.

'If I'm honest with you, you scared the hell out of me,' he admitted reluctantly. 'I'd only met you a few hours earlier and you'd already had this unimaginable effect on me.'

He still didn't understand how one person could have such an impact on another in so short a time.

'But surely that's what made it all the more exciting?' Thea frowned. 'It *was* intense—and unexpected, and a little scary—do you think I wasn't feeling just as overwhelmed as you? But I just ran with it. I wanted to see where it would take us.'

Ben shook his head. 'I don't *do* overwhelmed. I set a goal in life, put my head down, and work to achieve it.'

'So what about the passion, the spontaneity, the *fun*?'

'They're overrated,' he answered simply. 'That's why when I was walking you home I was telling myself I needed to back away from you. Instead I found I was wanting to meet you the next night, willing the time away before I could see you again. And then Dan opened that door and bellowed his head off.'

'That was just Daniel being Daniel—he'd have come around quickly enough,' Thea objected.

'I know. But it was the excuse I needed. That's why I had to walk away, there and then. And Dan knew me well enough to suspect why, so he let me do it. It was for your sake more than mine. Like I said, I wasn't a good match for you.'

He met her eyes, holding them steady, ignoring the look of disbelief which chased across her delicate features. Features which he could trace in his dreams—had reconstructed in his dreams even when he'd been redeployed. Even when he'd reminded himself that his life wasn't on Civvy Street—wasn't a safe life like Thea's. *His* life was working in war zones. And being the partner of someone who did that that was not a pleasant life.

He knew that from bitter experience.

Watching one person love with all their heart while the other stay closed off and unreachable was the most soul-destroying thing he knew. He could never have done that to Thea. He could never have made her happy. He would never have deserved her.

He hadn't banked on Dan dying less than two weeks

later. Lying in Ben's arms as the life drained out of him, choking out his last words to make Ben promise to take care of Thea. His best friend had gone, and for a short while he'd struggled to keep his emotions in check. The grief had almost overwhelmed him. It had taken every ounce of will-power to rein himself in, to stuff those feelings down and carry on with his life. What good would talking about it do?

'How do you know we weren't a good match?' Thea asked at last. 'Maybe I could have helped you. Aside from one date, you didn't really know me.'

'That's not true,' Ben told her. 'True, we'd never met be-fore, but I already knew what kind of a person you were. How strong you were. Dan used to talk about you all the time. He was so proud of you.'

Ben stared out of the window, as if remembering.

'I knew what you'd been through with your parents' death, and yet how caring, how open, how loyal you were. In no small part due to how close and supportive you and your brother were to each other. How much you share. *Shared.*'

Thea struggled to control an unexpected wave of sor-row. 'You mean unlike the way you *never* talk about your feelings?' she said sadly, worried about breaking this frag-ile moment.

'It's not what I do,' admitted Ben, seemingly lost in his own head.

'Why not?' She spoke gently, but he either couldn't hear her or didn't want to hear her.

Still, he was right, she realised. Physically, he might push himself way beyond anything his body should be doing at this stage—but *emotionally*? Emotionally was a whole different ball game. Ben barely even acknowledged his limitations to himself, let alone discussed the accident with her.

Had he always been this way? Was it something to do with the childhood Ben had had? From what little she knew of it, in his childhood he had been instilled with almost impossibly high expectations and a heavy sense of responsibility.

'You'd been through so much, and yet you'd managed to grow into a rounded, caring person.'

Ben continued to face out of the window, but she doubted he actually saw anything there.

'You supported your brother's career even though he told me you hated it, worrying every time he went to war about if he would come home. So I knew you deserved someone who could make you happy, and that certainly wasn't me. You didn't need the uncertainty, the instability, of a boyfriend who was a soldier too.'

'Wasn't that *my* choice?' Thea asked incredulously. 'And when we decided to get married anyway, wasn't that a good excuse for us to re-evaluate? See if it could be more than just a marriage of convenience?'

'We weren't meant to *be*, Thea. I'm not good at all this… *talking*.'

'You're not doing badly,' she noted. 'It's more than I've ever heard you admit before.'

'But you've had to push and push. We both know that would have grown old quickly—we'd have eventually grown to resent each other for it. And you would have been stifled in a cold marriage and never blossomed into the confident, successful doctor you are today.'

He'd only appreciated the truth of his words as they came out, and he was surprised when Thea nodded her head sadly.

'Funny, but I thought the same thing last night. I would never have realised how strong I really am.'

'So now we need to look to the future.' He changed the topic with forced brightness.

'Okay…' Thea acknowledged hesitantly. 'How do you propose we do that?'

'We try being friends—like you offered back at the hospital. We still have to live together whilst I'm recovering, so we need to find some solution—however temporary.'

She nodded slowly in agreement.

'Obviously there's still an attraction there,' he stated. After that spark the other morning there seemed little point denying it. Better to confront it head-on. 'But it's just a physical thing. We can ignore it if we really want to.'

And if he exhausted his body with physical exercise and took plenty of cold showers. But he didn't have a choice. He couldn't afford to let Thea get under his skin again or give in to temptation only to hurt her all over again when he backed away emotionally. And he would.

She looked as though she was going to object again, but then she closed her mouth and offered a tense smile.

'Sure we can ignore it. It's not as though it's even *real*, is it? Probably it's just a residual effect of a long-overdue conversation which, now we've had it, will go away by itself anyway. We've both moved on in five years, right?'

'Right,' he agreed, wondering why he felt as though a tiny black hole of emptiness had just opened up in his chest at the way she could dismiss it—*them*—so easily.

'Okay, so…friends,' she confirmed, licking her lips before chewing nervously on the inside of her cheek. 'And now, in the spirit of friendship, can I ask are you still going to push your recovery so hard? Push your body past its limits?'

'I don't know.' He didn't want to talk about it, but he forced himself to face her.

'You still think you'll return to active duty when you recover?'

'Sure.'

'I thought so. I said so to Sir James on the Board, when they told me to ask you to consider coming to work with the Air Ambulance.'

Not what he'd been expecting her to say.

He glanced at her sharply. Her feigned casual air wasn't fooling him.

'You want me to work with you?'

'The Board have asked me to present the offer to you. It would be on a consultancy basis. As they understand it, even though you're physically healed enough to return to work, you still won't be ready for deployment to a war zone again for quite a while. So working with the Air Ambulance would be a great way to keep your skills sharp.'

And it would keep him in the game if he was never cleared by the Army to return to active duty. He'd be damned if he was going to let his injuries defeat him. But he had to admit it *would* keep his skills honed. *Plus he'd get to work with Thea every day.*

He hastily pushed *that* thought to the back of his mind. 'What do you think?'

She shot him a penetrating look. 'You want to know what *I* think?'

She sounded so shocked it surprised him. It was as though she thought her opinion didn't matter to him. It couldn't be further from the truth.

He frowned at her. 'Of course. We'd be living together as well as working together. And you have to admit that it hasn't exactly been the easiest ride so far.'

'Of course,' she murmured.

For a moment he thought he caught an undercurrent of something. Then she went on.

'You're right. It hasn't been easy,' she began. 'But I can't imagine that being around the house all day, with little else to do but physio and more physio, is helping your medical brain. Plus there's no doubt you'll have trauma skills from being out there which we could really benefit from in Civvy Street.'

All of that was true, but it wasn't what Ben was interested in. He knew he was approaching dangerous territory—they were only just trying to forge a friendship—but he pushed the question anyway.

'What about the living and working together bit?' he prompted.

Again that tongue darted out to moisten dry lips, and Ben had to refocus before his brain started going down the wrong path once more.

She coughed, clearing her throat. 'I think it hasn't been easy, but we've been more open and honest with each other in the last two days than I think we've managed in five years. We're mature, successful professionals, and working together on a professional level should be fine. Plus my contract might not be renewed if I seem opposed to the proposal.'

'They *threatened* you?' So that was why she had been prepared to ask him. He felt disappointed, as well as angry. 'I'll have a word with them.'

She paused and swallowed hard.

'Best not to. Anyway they're right—you *would* be an asset. I think we ought to be able to put our personal feelings aside for medical gain.' She shrugged. 'There's only one other sticking point.'

'Which is…?' He didn't understand quite why it galled him that she should be so unemotional about it all.

'They all think we're…*reunited*, I suppose you could say.'

'We'd have to play a happily married couple,' Ben realised. 'How do you feel about that?'

'That bit…' She pulled a face. 'I'm not sure we could pull it off.'

He resisted the uncharacteristic impulse to suggest that they might have fun trying.

'You can tell them I'll think about it,' he told her at last. 'When are they thinking I would start?'

'How about during my next shift?'

* * *

'Jack, there's no way.' Thea felt panic rising, already bubbling in her throat. 'That's just *not* a good idea.'

'Sorry, Thea. That's what the boss said. Ben's on *your* team whilst you show him the ropes.'

'No!' She could have cried in despair.

'C'mon, Thea, I know you think that working with a partner can split your focus, but for what it's worth I've never known anyone as professional as you. And Major Abrams… *Ben*…has a formidable reputation. I don't think it's going to be as bad as you fear.'

Thea stared at Jack. His sincerity would have been touching if the entire situation hadn't been so terrifying. There was no way she could tell him the truth. She couldn't tell *any* of her colleagues. She and Ben had started their 'happily reunited' charade last week—now they had to live up to that.

Talk about impossible.

She had never taken a sick day in her life. Never missed a single day of work. But right now it was all she could do not to drop everything and run straight through the door to the car park and freedom.

She'd hoped to call Ben's bluff about not having any problem with him working there, and she'd been surprised when he'd accepted the temporary role. But she'd taken comfort in the fact that at least they wouldn't be working together.

That, she'd decided, would be a step too far.

And yet here he was, on his first day, assigned to her team. How were they possibly meant to work together when neither of them could bear to be in the other's company for long? Ever since the pancakes, and their agreement to give friendship a go, they'd made a concerted effort to make small-talk and go out running together. Their strained conversation had been painful and draining. Work had been a welcome escape.

But now they were expected to work together.

Anything else she might have said to Jack stuck in her throat as Ben rounded the corner. She squared her shoulders, conscious of Jack watching them, and strived to regulate her laboured breathing. She had to keep it together.

'What do you need me to do, Boss?'

Polite and deferential—all part of his Army training—but her throat was nevertheless too dry for her to answer. The idea of being boss to Dr Ben Abrams would have been a daunting prospect at the best of times, let alone given all the baggage between the two of them.

'Boss...?'

She heard the gentle prompting in his tone. Jack didn't know Ben well enough to pick up on it, but she knew Ben was trying to encourage her. She was both grateful and resentful at the same time.

'You remember Ron and Andy? My paramedics?'

'Yeah, and Harry, our pilot,' Ben confirmed. 'I've just been to introduce myself to them all again.'

Of course he had, she bristled. He might appear deferential, but he was used to running the show. How was he going to respond to taking orders from *her*? Because she *would* be giving them. That much *had* changed in five years. This was *her* team and *she* was responsible for what went on in the field during her watch. She took that responsibility seriously and she had her own way of doing things. A way which suited her guys.

Two bosses vying to take charge. Now what? How was this possibly going to work?

'Thea—new call-out,' Jack cut in with sudden efficiency as he slipped his headphones from around his neck to cover his head. 'Sounds like a horse rider fell—the road ambulance have requested our assistance.'

Well, it seemed as though she was about to find out.

With a rush of adrenalin lending her strength, Thea turned her focus to the screen to read the incoming transcript. There was an open fracture to the ankle, hence the request for a trauma doctor. It didn't take her long to make a decision, and she spun around to Ben.

'Alert Andy and Harry and grab the gear. There won't be enough seats if we have to transport anyone, so tell Ron he can monitor from here. Meet you at the heli.'

'Understood.' Ben issued the automatic verbal confirmation before ducking out of the door.

'Send the co-ordinates to the chopper, Jack, and update me with anything as we're in flight.'

'Roger.' Jack dipped his head.

Racing out into the corridor, Thea grabbed her own kit and headed out onto the Tarmac, swinging up into her seat just moments behind the others.

'Harry—you've met Ben already, I understand? He's a military trauma surgeon, recently returned from Afghanistan,' Thea stated, as soon as Harry had completed his checks and they were airborne. It was a discreet attempt to establish herself as team leader.

'Yeah, turns out we served in the same region a couple of years ago.' Harry smiled. 'Although we never met out there.'

Another veteran who no doubt knew of Ben's reputation. Thea couldn't help another small stab of apprehension. If Harry knew Ben in a professional capacity she might have to work even harder to ensure she didn't end up losing control of her own team. It was almost out of her hands. The dynamics of the team largely depended, whether she liked it or not, on how well Ben could take orders from her.

'Keep a look-out as we approach the scene and stay alert,' Thea advised Ben over the headset. 'The rider was apparently on a hack alongside a canal, so when we get closer we'll follow the canal and look for somewhere to land. By the map it looks like there are some accessible fields nearby. You can learn a lot from the scene with a bird's-eye view like this.'

'Acknowledged.'

No doubt he already knew all that, from his military training, but so far he didn't appear to be trying to take command—subconsciously or not.

'Approaching scene,' Harry confirmed about ten minutes later.

'Rapid response vehicles, eleven o'clock,' Thea observed.

'Noted.'

As Harry checked the area for safe landing sites and brought the chopper gently down, Thea waited for the thumbs-up before nodding to her team and jumping to the ground.

She covered the distance to the casualty quickly, taking in everything around them as she introduced herself and her team to the patient and offered some brief reassurance. A quick visual confirmed the leg injury.

'Open fracture above the ankle.'

'Right.' Ben nodded grimly.

His jaw had locked, and she knew he had the same concerns as her. Open fractures to the ankle were often associated with a lack of blood supply to the foot, which could result in the loss of the foot itself. Like her, he must be running through ways to protect the blood supply.

Still, before focussing all her attention on the obvious injury she wanted to ensure that there wasn't another, less obvious but potentially more life-threatening, injury to prioritise. Distracted by the open wound, the road crew might have missed potentially fatal internal bleeding into the patient's chest, his pelvis or his stomach.

To her surprise Ben, as though anticipating her immediate priority, stepped away to the rider's girlfriend, to ask what had happened, as she took the opportunity to ask the rider himself. Her account might shed light on something the patient himself had missed—like the angle of his fall. It might help Thea to decide if there was another test she needed to carry out.

After running through her checks Thea stepped away to discuss a treatment plan with Andy. Ben quickly joined them.

'A startled duck took sudden flight off the canal, spooking his horse. The horse bucked and the rider fell onto the gravelly, tree-root-riddled path,' Ben advised.

'I got the same account.' Thea nodded. 'Plus he was clear, concise and calm. My gut says that although he's in some pain, there are no underlying issues. He's stable.'

'Agreed.'

'That blood supply concerns me,' she murmured. 'I want to try an open reduction before we move him.'

'Good plan, but you're going to need some strong pain relief if you want to get that bone back under the skin,' Ben noted.

'I'll get the Ketamine,' Andy said, jogging back to the helicopter.

'That's a pretty powerful drug.' Ben looked surprised. 'I didn't know emergency vehicles carried it.'

'The road ambulances don't,' Thea agreed. The drug could effectively unplug a patient's sight, hearing—the lot. 'But it's another advantage of the Air Ambulance having trauma doctors. We can carry a range of equipment and drugs other rapid responders can't.'

'Nice.' Ben looked impressed. 'So is that why the road crew called us out instead of just packing the rider into the ambulance and taking him to hospital?'

'Yep.' Thea busied herself getting her kit together to perform the reduction procedure. 'The road crew can only scoop and run, whilst with our knowledge and our kit we can, as they say, stay and play. Treating an injury like this in the field can mean the difference between the foot needing to be amputated and saving it.'

'Right…' Ben nodded in agreement. 'It's a very battlefield-orientated approach.'

Thea blushed. Of course he would already know that

as well as anyone. Still, he wasn't rolling his eyes or complaining at the lesson. Perhaps her initial fears about them working together were unfounded. And it felt good to be in control of something—of Ben—when up until half an hour ago she'd been feeling as if she was drowning.

'Exactly. Right, I'm going to update them back at base. Do you want to go and explain to the rider what we're about to give him and why?'

'Sure.'

Ben jogged off immediately and Thea contacted Jack. She couldn't help noticing a slight stiffness in his gait. The cold weather, she realised instinctively. She'd noticed he always seemed to be in that bit more pain when the temperature dropped, or if a storm was brewing. He was like a human barometer.

As she checked in with Jack she took the opportunity to snag a high-vis puffer jacket from the helicopter, and she tossed it to Ben as she returned to the rider.

'I need you to go to the end of the lane when you've finished with the patient and flag down the second road crew who are on their way. Put that on and they'll see you better.'

She studiously ignored Ben's sharp look as she administered pain relief to the patient, but noticed that he was quick to wriggle into the jacket's cosiness. The pain must have been twisting into his bones.

She sat back thoughtfully for a moment whilst the drug took effect. Ben had turned towards the rider, and his reassuring voice was repeating information to ensure the guy understood.

'Okay, so Ketamine's what we call a dissociative drug. It's going to make you feel a little strange, maybe a little spaced out, and you might not remember any of this—all right?'

The patient muttered something which she didn't catch, but Ben was clearly completely in control.

'It's going to take your pain away and enable us to do

our job. We're going to try to save that foot.' Ben glanced up as Thea took the ankle and gave him the nod. 'Okay, are you ready?'

Confident that Ben had the rider's trust and attention, Thea knew all she needed to do was get on with her job. With any luck she would have five, maybe six minutes to reduce the open fracture. If the patient wasn't compliant, she would have to administer a second dose.

'Just try to relax,' Ben soothed the rider. 'This stuff will work much better if you're relaxed.'

Andy and Ron were both good, and she was proud of her team, but there was no doubt that Ben had an extra edge. It wasn't just his Army training, or his skill as a trauma surgeon, it was something essentially *Ben*. He was still talking to the patient, looking up to give her a brief nod when he saw the drug was starting to work at the same moment as she was already moving in to work on the ankle. They seemed to be completely in sync.

Working carefully and quickly, she tried the procedure, but the man was becoming agitated, and with only a look to Ben Thea was able to confirm that the rider wasn't responding adequately to the drug. She wouldn't be trying a second time.

Ben left to flag down the second road crew whilst she stabilised the rider for transportation to hospital, since they had been unable to reduce the wound on site.

As they flew back to the base Thea couldn't help admiring Ben. It was odd, but the ease and harmony the two of them lacked in their personal relationship had appeared automatically within the first hour of their professional one.

CHAPTER EIGHT

FOR THE FOURTH time in as many minutes Ben tried to read an interesting article in his newspaper, but he found his eyes wandering back to the glass wall which separated himself and Thea. Just as they had been doing more and more frequently since he'd started working with the Air Ambulance less than a week ago.

If he'd thought their working and living together would drive a much-needed wedge between them, dampen his emotions and desires, then he'd been completely wrong. All it had shown him was that Thea really was incredible. Dedicated, focussed and skilled, with a knowledge base a doctor twice her age would be proud of. She quietly commanded loyalty and respect from her team—and the other teams, too—and gave it back in spades. And Ben knew he wasn't the only one to think so.

In spite of all that had happened to her—losing her parents as a kid, losing Dan, and then his own actions—Thea had held tight to her resolve and grown into a kind woman and an extraordinary trauma doctor. And he felt proud of her even though she'd done it all on her own. It was getting harder and harder to keep his distance, but he knew he had nothing to offer her and she deserved so much.

He watched as Thea reappeared from the kitchen, making her way to the rec room area, where various other team members sat relaxing. She flopped down sideways onto an easy chair and threw her legs—long, sexy legs, even clad in her flight suit—over the chunky chair-arm, before tucking into a yoghurt with a sense of relief.

'Voracious appetite!' Nic teased her, and despite himself Ben set down his paper and sauntered casually over, just as Thea replied.

'Yeah, well, having had nothing but paperwork to do all morning, the very second I decided to grab lunch there was, of course, a call-out. Now I'm starving.'

'And *that's* the extent of your lunch?' Ben frowned as he sank down with careful nonchalance in the chair next to Thea.

'Are you kidding?' She snorted, jerking her head back over her shoulder. 'I inhaled a pulled pork sandwich before I even left that kitchen.'

'Hey, that was mine!' Harry stopped tapping on his phone long enough to look up.

'Sorry, mate—first come, first served.' Thea grinned. 'You were on a call-out.'

'Oh, yeah...' He pulled a face. 'A fourteen-year-old swimmer at a meet—bad dive, landed on her head. Probably permanent spinal injury, unfortunately, poor kid. I'm kidding about the sandwich, by the way. I brought enough in for everybody.'

'Yeah, I know.' Thea smiled. 'I heard you tell everyone this morning.'

The banter continued and Ben smiled at the easy camaraderie. It was what had made it so easy for him to slip into his new role—feeling instantly accepted and welcome. It would be a shame to leave. He'd thoroughly enjoyed his first couple of days with Thea, and now working with Team Two was proving almost as enjoyable.

When he'd first realised Nic was the trauma doctor in charge of Team Two he'd had his reservations, but it turned out Nic was a good leader and a skilled doctor, with the same strong ethos as the soldiers Ben had worked alongside in combat. Working with the new team was proving enjoyable as well as informative; it was clear that whatever had happened between Thea and Nic was firmly in the past—for both parties.

He knew it shouldn't please him that Thea had no love interest. It wasn't his business and it shouldn't have any bearing on him whatsoever. Yet whenever he watched her Ben couldn't help feeling…what? Contentment? Pride? Maybe even a hint of healthy possessiveness?

He shook his head. He had no business feeling either of them. His Army Medical Board assessment was a matter of weeks away and then he would be shipped out to another combat zone. Back to actual trauma surgery in the field, to that rush of adrenalin, the pressure, the buzz.

Funny, but the thought of it seemed to have lost its ability to give him that same high it once had.

He glanced across at Thea. No more having to feign being a happily married couple in front of everyone. That should be a *good* thing. Only over the last few days it had felt less and less like such a charade. The air had been significantly cleared between them, and ever since he'd admitted to his old feelings for Thea it seemed to have paved the way for them to cultivate the beginnings of a real friendship, much to his surprise. If only he could keep control of the lust, which seemed harder to resist with each passing day.

Thea was intelligent and fun and witty, as well as being stunningly beautiful. He enjoyed being around her to listen to her, talk to her, work with her. The feelings had crept up on him, slowly at first, and now he found himself actively seeking her out, feeling pleased when she seemed to come looking for him, too.

He tuned back in to the conversation just as Ron was urging Thea to join them at the pub.

'Sorry, Doc, no crying off—this one is mandatory.'

'Since when is going to the pub mandatory?'

Thea tried to laugh it off, but Ben could see those tiny

stress lines of hers—imperceptible to anyone else—tightening around her eyes.

'Since we've been working together for a couple of years, and not one of us here knew you were married.' Ron feigned hurt. 'Let alone to *sod-that-for-a-game-of-soldiers* Major Abrams, here.'

Ben would have laughed if Thea hadn't suddenly gone so tense. Unexpectedly he experienced an instinctive urge to protect her.

'You know what it's like with us soldiers...' He reached casually across Thea to the fruit bowl and snagged an apple, temporarily creating a human buffer for her. 'You never know where we are, what mission we're on, when we'll be coming home—and you know what people are like for asking questions. Even well-intentioned. Sometimes you can feel a bit daft when the only answer you can give is, *I don't know.*'

Ron looked thoughtful. 'I never thought of it like that. I suppose you *would* feel a bit like you were always in the dark. Can't be pleasant.'

'It isn't,' Thea confirmed.

She cast Ben a grateful glance, which filled him with an unexpected warmth. Lots of the little things that Thea did were causing that reaction these days—from a shared, knowing smile to a grateful glance like that one. He knew he should be taking it as a warning, forcing more space between them. But instead he was doing the opposite.

'Well, that aside, the guys were talking before and we want to know what *else* we don't know about our devilish Doc Abrams, here.' Ron unpeeled his banana and gulped down half of it in one mouthful.

'Hmm, well, let me think... I'm a whizz in the kitchen,' retorted Ben promptly, and the group chuckled.

'Sorry, mate, we mean the *other* Doc Abrams.' Ron chuckled, polishing off the rest of the fruit.

'Right,' said Andy. 'We reckon it's time to find out.'

'I'm not sure I like the sound of this…' Thea feigned a frown at her friend.

'Nah—you will,' Andy assured her. 'We've got a couple of days off from tomorrow night—how about we all go for a drink after work?'

'Plus it's time for you guys to tell us what's been going on,' Ron added pointedly. 'And, Ben, we'll tell you all the little fun stories we've got about your wife here.'

'What stories?' Thea wrinkled her nose.

Ron smiled broadly. 'Like the fact that the first time she travelled on the chopper she threw up!'

'Really?' Ben turned to Thea as she turned beetroot-red. But at least she was starting to relax a little now the very personal questions were over.

'Thanks for the loyalty, guys. *Not*.'

'Come on, Ben, you're new to the crew,' urged Franco, another paramedic. 'It's a good way to get to know everyone without the stress of call-outs.'

Ben turned to Thea. 'I reckon a night out would do us both good.'

He knew it wasn't really her thing, and it wasn't really his either, but it seemed like a good opportunity to try and create that distance he was considering. It would certainly beat going back to the cottage together and tiptoeing around her in the kitchen in an effort not to simply drag her into his arms and pin her back against the kitchen island.

'Then tomorrow night it is,' Ron confirmed, pleased when everyone nodded their agreement.

But when nobody was watching Thea shot Ben a confused glance, as though somehow he'd managed to upset her again. Before he could catch her attention to find out, another paramedic came running around the corner.

'RTC just called in, guys. Big one. They're asking for both Air Ambulances.'

'Two? Hell, must be bad.' Nic was up and moving before the paramedic had time to say more. Everyone else was right on his heels.

'I want my whole team,' Nic instructed as the two teams raced out onto the tarmac. 'Franco, don't stay behind this time—and, Ben, you're coming too. Sounds like we could do with an extra trauma doc, and one of us can always ride in the road ambulance if necessary.'

Thea stood up from her fourth collision victim, circling her arm and stretching her neck from one side to the other. She had been working non-stop for the last few hours, first triaging, then tending. Her latest victim had a collapsed left thorax, both clavicles and numerous ribs broken, and Thea had been particularly concerned about internal aortic bleeding which might ultimately prove fatal. Until the other trauma team returned to airlift the woman to hospital Thea had been draining the chest cavity, but she knew she was just fighting to buy the woman enough time to get there.

With even a third team now here, she should transfer the woman to their care, and move on to the next casualty who urgently needed her help. Ron had already called her over a couple of times for the next one on their priority list—a list which just kept getting longer as they carefully extricated more victims from their cars. She, Ben and Nic were staying on site to stabilise as many as they could either for air transport or transfer by road crew, but it felt like a losing battle.

As she signalled to another trauma doctor she averted her eyes from the black bags dotted around. The accident had been horrific. Multiple cars—or what had once passed for cars—were scattered over a good mile of motorway, along with debris, people screaming for help, and those who were ominously quiet.

As they'd approached from the air the sheer scale of the collision had been evident, with the police struggling to close all six lanes of the motorway and clear the way. The biggest threat, however, was the two cars still smouldering despite efforts to control them. The fire brigade was still fighting to reach them up the packed motorway.

Both air teams had got to work as soon as they had landed, assessing and operating in tandem with the four rapid response vehicles which *had* made it through the traffic, with more on their way all the time. Working quickly, Thea had confirmed a spinal injury, a dislocated knee, a hip injury and a head injury, continually communicating with both Nic and Ben in order for them to assess the priority patients.

She prepared herself now to move on to her fifth casualty.

'I think I've got the driver of the van,' Thea calculated. 'They've managed to get him out of the vehicle now, and initial assessment shows he has definite internal bleeding.'

'I'm still with my motorcyclist.' Nic ran across the motorway. 'Ben took the woman with the head injury.'

'Acknowledged.'

'Whoever finishes first should move on to the passenger of that second car, though. They're getting her out now, and I don't like the way she's progressing.'

'Understood,' Thea nodded, jogging to her driver and treating him as best she could before she bumped him to the top of the medevac list.

Ben appeared at her side without warning.

'Take over my patient,' he instructed, his voice oddly quiet.

'Where are *you* going?' Obediently Thea headed over to take his place, but Ben didn't respond. Instead he raced towards the evacuated area where small fires still burned as the fire engines inched closer and closer through the backed-up traffic which was blocking even the hard shoulder with damaged vehicles hit by debris earlier on.

Where a car had been smouldering before, Thea could now see flames jumping and dancing and she realised it could blow at any time. *What the hell was Ben thinking, running in there?*

She ran forward to intercept him, thinking he mustn't have realised, but he almost mowed her down as he sprinted past her and into the danger zone.

'*Ben!*' Thea shouted. 'You can't go in there.'

He ignored her, seemingly oblivious. It was useless. Ben either couldn't—or wouldn't—hear her. But the look on his face as he'd run past her had chilled Thea to her core. His expression had been one she didn't recognise. A dangerous look, almost as if he hadn't even seen her. Hadn't necessarily even seen what she was seeing.

Dr Fields had said months ago that Ben's PTSD was only mild, but was this an escalation? She saw the body bags with fresh eyes, through *Ben's* eyes, wondering if they had triggered something for him.

Bang.

Thea screamed as a piece of flying debris landed a couple of metres behind Ben. He launched forward to protect her body, pushing her further away from the demarcation line and, mercifully bringing himself out of the danger area.

'Stay out of here,' he ordered, his voice oddly strangulated.

'Ben, we don't have time for this,' she argued desperately. 'You have your head injury casualty, and I have to get to my van driver.'

Boom.

One of the cars exploded and the sound was deafening. Thea barely had time to react before Ben threw her to the ground, his body covering hers. She heard the sound of metal slamming into the ground. Felt the Tarmac vibrate. But with Ben over her she had no idea how near or far the debris had fallen.

Then he was up, lifting her bodily into the air and throwing her well clear. The haunted look was more pronounced than ever. Then he was gone. Racing to the exploded car and dropping to the ground as he got closer to the intense heat. He began to move forward on his belly and elbows.

'Ben!'

He crawled closer and closer to the flames. A loud *bang* came from the burning engine. There was going to be another explosion and there was absolutely nothing she could do to save Ben.

Nic ran to the edge of the zone, his hands cupped around his mouth as he bellowed Ben's name.

'What the hell is he *thinking*?' Nic sounded frantic.

'I think its PTSD,' Thea whispered. This was why she'd needed to be there for Ben when he was discharged. Someone to talk to. But she hadn't helped him. She hadn't encouraged him to open up enough.

Why did the idea upset her so much? Because she'd thought they'd been getting on so well lately? Because she'd genuinely thought he was changing in the way he saw her, how much he trusted her?

And now he was in there, in the danger zone, risking his life. *For what?* She *still* didn't understand him. It scared her.

'I don't know.' Thea bit her lip. 'He was working on that woman with the head injury one minute, then racing over there looking like death the next. A paramedic is still with her, and another is with my van driver, but we needs to get over there.'

Nic nodded grimly. 'Right, I'll go with you and check on them.'

Tearing her eyes from the last spot where she'd seen Ben, Thea ducked her head and raced after Nic. She didn't have time for emotion, or these thoughts. She had patients— people who needed her and who *wanted* her help. Not like Ben. She needed to focus on them.

Nic looked up at her as she approached. 'She keeps slipping in and out of consciousness. Apparently she was thrown clear of her car, but she had a two-month-old daughter in the back. Ben's risking his life trying to save that woman's baby.'

'She has a *baby*?'

Thea felt numb. The irony wasn't lost on her. It was as if all the fates were taunting her that she was judging Ben right now, but she still hadn't been entirely honest herself. She felt a gurgle of hysterical laughter bubble up, *so* unlike her, and hastily swallowed it back down.

It must have been all over her face because Nic suddenly grabbed her hand, snapping her back into focus. 'Yeah,' he squeezed her hand quickly, as if to offer her comfort.

He didn't know about the baby, but could he read her thoughts? See the guilt etched in her face?

'If Ben's going to give his life trying to save the baby, the least you can do is fight to save the mum. I'll take your van driver.'

Nodding, but unable to speak, Thea took over.

'Try not to worry. Ben must know what he's doing—he's a soldier. He's trained to risk his life for others. I understand how scared you must be right now, it's obvious how much you love him, but put it out of your head and focus,' Nic advised gently.

He was right. She *was* still in love with Ben. After all this time she was no closer to getting over him than she had been five years ago. Well, she was damned if she was going to let fear take her over. Shutting out the black thoughts, Thea forced herself to work, to concentrate on the casualty in front of her, who had passed out again.

Head down, forcing herself not to be distracted, she worked steadily on the young woman, relieved when she'd alleviated the pressure in the patient's chest and the mother of the baby finally regained consciousness.

'Van driver's stable. I'll take over here.' Nic suddenly appeared and drew her to one side. 'Go and check on Ben.

See if he's saved the baby. If not try to get him out of there. Then move on to the next casualty.'

'Understood,' Thea choked out, hoping her legs wouldn't buckle under her as she stood up.

He was still over there? How long had it been?

Thea gratefully passed the reins on to Nic and raced to the edge of the danger area. The remaining vehicle creaked and groaned distressingly. It sounded as if it was about to blow up at any moment. She resisted the urge to vomit.

'Ben, you have to get out of there!' she cried again. *'Ben!'*

She waited for what seemed like an eternity, and just as she was about to run to her next victim Thea saw his feet, then his legs, as he emerged painfully slowly.

'Get out of there!' she yelled.

Finally free of the wreckage, he stood up—and only then did she see the baby wrapped in his arms. Emotions tore through her without warning. Fear, relief, and the searing agony of the loss of her own baby—*their* own baby.

'There's a pulse!' Ben shouted this confirmation, tearing out of the area as another bang—louder this time—could be heard. 'Didn't you say Nic had extensive paediatric experience?'

'Give her to me.' Nic had already raced over and Ben willingly handed over the bundle. 'Nice going, Ben. That baby's only alive because of what you've just done.'

Words froze in Thea's mouth. She wanted to tell him how stupid he had been. But watching the tiny baby being raced safely away in Nic's arms stopped the words from coming out. Instead she pressed her palms to her eyes, stemming the tears.

'Are you okay?' she managed, just as they heard a *whoosh* followed by a *boom*. Ben swept her into his arms and charged them both backwards. By the time he released her the car he'd crawled out from, carrying the precious bundle, was a fireball, and smoke was billowing out around the scene. All the debris, however, was still within the danger zone. A metre-long shard of metal had been driven into the ground exactly where Ben had been standing with the baby a few moments earlier.

'I'm fine.'

Ben had dismissed her concerns. It felt as though he was dismissing *her*, in a way he never did with anyone else.

'Who's left to triage?' he asked.

CHAPTER NINE

'To Ben,' Franco announced quietly, raising his pint glass. 'If it hadn't been for his actions yesterday that baby wouldn't be stable in hospital with his mother now.'

'Ben,' chorused the remainder of the two teams soberly.

Ben grunted but said nothing, trying to temper his displeasure. They had no idea how much he hated this. The undeserved praise. They had no idea how many lives he'd lost, how many dead bodies on the battlefield, men he'd failed to save. He was just lucky he'd got to the baby in time. Which was more than could be said for Dan.

He downed his drink in record time and took the opportunity of going to the bar for a refill just so that he could slip away for a few minutes to clear his head. He'd barely got his drink when a soft, female body pushed against him.

'On the hard stuff, I see,' Thea murmured, looking at the glass of water in his hand.

The crowd around the bar was three rows deep, and she didn't exactly have the physique to push her way through. He pointed out as much.

'Elbows.' She smiled, holding them up as if for him to inspect. 'And stop deflecting.'

'I just don't like the accolades,' he admitted. 'I don't deserve them.'

'Yesterday was horrible—we lost a lot of patients. We don't even know if those we got to hospital will make it,' Thea pointed out gently. 'But you're the one who risked his life to crawl into burning wreckage for a baby who might not have even been there.'

'So we cheer that and forget the bad?' Ben pulled a face.

'No, we find a small victory in a hellish situation and celebrate *that*,' she told him quietly. 'Are you telling me that you never did that in all your time out in Afghanistan?'

Yeah, they'd definitely done that. *He'd* done that. Until it had been *him* they were celebrating. Then it hadn't seemed so…appropriate.

Still, her calm reminder had eased the tension he'd been feeling. She'd made him feel stronger again. The crowd surged slightly and Ben pulled her towards him protectively, concerned about her getting pushed too hard. She barely resisted before slipping neatly into his arms.

Too neatly. As if she was meant to be there. They both stayed still, taking comfort in the closeness, the crush and clamour fading away until all he was really aware of was himself and Thea. It felt particularly intimate, and he knew that the tension of the day, the memories, meant he'd let his guard down. Suddenly he didn't care.

'Can I get you a drink?' he asked softly. *Could she hear his heartbeat accelerate?*

'I have one.' She shook her head, but her voice sounded unusually throaty and he wondered if she was as aware of him as he was of her.

'Thea—'

'Can I ask you something—?'

They spoke at the same time, both stopping and offering a nervous laugh.

'Go ahead,' Ben said eventually, not caring about the crowd surging around them.

It occurred to him to ask Thea if she wanted to go somewhere quiet to talk, but he didn't want to break the spell, and thought that maybe the crowd was somehow making her feel more secure than if it had just been the two of them. Too much pressure.

'What happened yesterday?' she asked tentatively.

He huffed out a hard breath. It wasn't exactly a surprise question, but that didn't make it any easier. Still, he was determined to be honest with her. They'd come so far he didn't want to mess it up now. He cast around for the right words before realising there were none. There was just the truth.

'Your PTSD is triggered at night, when the house is silent, right? What triggered it at that crash site yesterday?

He assessed her thoughtfully.

'I think seeing everything from the air definitely reminded me of my own accident. But instead of making me freeze it cut out my fears and drove me to act on autopilot, without really knowing what I was doing.'

'But you ran into an evacuated zone; you could have been blown up,' Thea objected, still concerned.

'I know that. I knew it then. But when my patient told me her baby was still in there... I couldn't *not*.' How could he explain it any other way? 'Standing back just isn't *me*.'

'And if that car had blown up and you'd be in there you'd have both died.'

The shake in her voice touched his heart. Without thinking he pulled her into his arms and held her close.

'And if it had blown up and I hadn't even tried how could I have lived with myself?'

'At least you'd have been alive,' Thea muttered against his chest.

But he could tell by her tone that she was glad he'd saved the baby. Glad he was the kind of soldier who was willing to make that sacrifice if it was the right thing to do.

He pulled her in even tighter for a moment, breathing in the crisp, clean scent of her shampoo which he recognised so well from the shower room. Everything about Thea was like a breath of fresh air. And now she was opening up more to him, just because he had been honest with her. At least partly. He wasn't sure how to be completely honest without letting her down, but for the first time in five years he wanted to change, to find a way to be in her life.

Ben frowned as darker thoughts crept into his head. His memories of that IED hadn't been as controlled as he'd led Thea to believe. The motorway crash site had triggered other memories of his accident. Memories which had crowded his brain, gripped his chest, almost making him incapable of breathing. Even now the images were sneaking back in. He wasn't ready to face them yet, and before they could take root he hastily shut them down.

But he couldn't afford to do that because that meant shutting Thea out too, and hadn't he just decided he wanted to change—for her? Which meant he needed to talk to her, to tell her. Yet he didn't know how. He only knew he'd felt utter fear and panic when Thea had been standing so close to that car when it exploded.

'I couldn't cope with anything ever happening to you.'

It wasn't until he caught sight of her face, flushed with pleasure as she stared up at him, that he realised he had uttered the thought aloud.

'Really?'

It made him feel good that his words affected her so positively.

'Not like you to be lost for words,' he teased, raising his hand to push a few stray tendrils of hair from her face. 'Anything else you want to know?'

She shook her head.

'Anything you want to tell *me*, then?'

She shook her head again, her eyes flickering to his mouth and back up to his eyes. As if she was waiting for him to kiss her. As if she *wanted* him to kiss her.

His gut kicked harder than a fifty-calibre machine gun recoil. Only it felt much more pleasant.

'Nothing at all?' He tried to tease her as he fought to slow his accelerating pulse.

'Okay...well, for the record, you cook really, *really* well.' She laughed softly. 'I never knew that before.'

'There's a lot we don't know about each other,' he reminded her gently. 'But I'd like to change that.'

Her eyes widened for a moment. 'I'd like that too.'

'Good.'

Before she could say anything else he cupped her cheek, dipping his head down and brushing her lips gently with his.

Her response was tentative, and then she was sliding her hands around his back, but not holding too tight.

He cautioned himself about pushing her too fast. He took his time pulling her closer to him, all the while exploring her mouth delicately. Afraid of startling her.

But a few moments later Thea seemed to have her own ideas. Her hands were sliding up his spine with confidence, holding tighter as she pulled herself in closer and pushed her body up against his.

He deepened the kiss, feeling lust jolt through him as she met his tongue boldly with hers. The kiss became unhurried, and boundless, and sensual. It reached deep inside him, making him for one long moment forget everything else. Around them, all the bustle and revelry faded away.

It was several long moments before they surfaced, but he couldn't drag his eyes from her face.

'So, where do we go from here?'

'How about straight home?' she couldn't help suggesting, her cheeks flushing slightly at her own audaciousness.

The whole way home Thea could barely believe her boldness. But it had been as though Ben was deliberately holding himself back, trying to be gentle with her, and she didn't want that at all.

She'd only slept with three other men besides Ben. One before him, which had been her fumbling, cringeworthy first time—and second time. Then two after Ben. But whether it had been because of Ben, or the miscarriage, those relationships hadn't stood a chance, and although the sex had been fine it hadn't been all fireworks and crashing waves.

She'd been beginning to wonder if there was something wrong with her. But just that kiss with Ben had set her body on fire, from her toes up, and now she felt more daring than she'd ever wanted to be before.

The taxi ride was like a lesson in pure torment, as Ben drew lazy circles on her arm and her back, occasionally dropping gentle kisses on her lips, but not letting them get too close for fear of losing control and giving the driver an X-rated show.

By the time she tumbled out of the taxi she was shaking with lust and pent-up tension. It was only as she was walking up to the door that she felt a momentary pang of nerves, but then Ben slid his hand to the small of her back and guided her into the house, closing the door behind them. He pulled her against him, one hand sliding into her hair to tilt her head up to his, his lips claiming hers with all the confidence and expertise she expected from him. Her nerves forgotten, Thea gave herself up to him.

She felt his reaction hard against her thigh, and a bubble of impatience popped inside her stomach as she reached down to fumble with his belt. She'd never felt this impatient with anyone before, but right now all she wanted was to take him in her hand, feel that velvety smoothness against her palm.

'You're sure?'

Ben broke off for a moment to pull back, and Thea felt the beginnings of a confidence she'd never had before.

'Will you just shut up and kiss me?' she muttered, slightly abashed, reaching for his jeans and undoing the buttons until he sprang out, revelling in his low moan of appreciation when she slid her fingers around him.

Following her pace, Ben divested her of her tee shirt and bra in a couple of smooth movements, before snaking

one arm around her waist, the other hand expertly caress-
ing her breast. Then, arching her back slightly, he bent his
head to bestow a trail of hot kisses down the line of her
neck to one hard nipple, before taking it in his mouth and
sucking deeply until she gasped aloud. His tongue slipped
in and out, deftly flicking over the bud before taking it into
his mouth once again. Then he turned his attention to the
other breast, and she could feel him flexing in her palm
as she threw her head back to push her nipple further into
his mouth.

'Let's take this next door,' Ben murmured, shifting out
of her hand and lifting her up, wrapping her legs around
him so he could carry her.

'Not upstairs?' Thea felt uncertainty creeping back.

'Too far.' He shook his head in mock contrition and she
felt any doubts dissipate.

Lowering them both swiftly down onto the rug, he slid
her jeans off, hooked a finger under her lace panties before running it between her legs. She moaned, sounding
out his name, and he repeated the action, this time dipping
his finger in, making her squirm with pleasure.

He didn't even have his tee shirt off and hazily Thea
reached for it, wanting him as naked as she was. Wanting
to feel his skin slide across hers. But he'd already ducked
away, his mouth moving down from her straining nipple
to her stomach.

'I want to taste you,' he murmured, his tongue leaving a
gentle whorl on her belly button, his kisses weaving lower
and lower down her abdomen.

Filled with lust, her bottom shifting against his touch,
Thea didn't even realise he'd slipped her panties off until
his tongue chased up the inside of one thigh, gliding over
her and flicking through her wetness, making her pelvis
jolt in response.

'Ben…' Thea gasped. 'What about you?'

'Relax,' Ben murmured against the sensitive skin, making her throb and swell with need. 'Right now this is about *you.*'

Something jarred slightly in the recesses of her head, but before she had time to think Ben was cupping her backside with his hands, pushing his tongue inside her, drawing back only to suck before sliding in again.

She grasped the rug for traction. It had never been like this for her before, and her head was swimming with building need.

'Thea, you're perfect. So hot, so wet…' he murmured. 'So close…'

'Don't stop,' begged Thea, arching up to him, loving it that he so obligingly returned to the task in hand.

He pushed his tongue in deeper, then moved back to suck a little harder, and instinctively she tilted her hips up to encourage him. Her hands moved to touch his shoulders, frustrated by the feel of fabric instead of bare skin, and she slid her fingers into his hair instead.

His tongue moved faster, making her catch her breath, wanting more, then demanding more. She instinctively opened her legs a little wider and he groaned, the sound vibrating against her body. It was her undoing.

The orgasm started slowly, with her fingers and toes tingling first, then quickly picked up pace as it spread through her veins like fire and tore through her, making her cry out as her body was caught up in waves of bliss. But Ben wasn't stopping. He held her writhing hips in place, his tongue never leaving her as he kept up his relentless pace, and Thea gave herself up to a return wave which ripped through her abdomen and made her body tremble. Even as she came down the aftershocks kept pulsing through her, leaving her fighting to breathe and unable to speak.

She'd wanted fireworks—he'd given her a New Year's Eve grandstand. How was she ever to repay the debt?

It was going to take her a few minutes longer to regain

her breath, and she was grateful when Ben came up to lie beside her and pull her into his arms. Her hand crept over him, grazing down his front to where his jeans were still open. She slipped her hand inside.

His reaction was immediate, and the guttural sound he made turned her on again. Already.

Thea smiled shyly at him, barely able to believe they'd turned such a corner. Hardly daring to think this might be the start of something else.

She pushed herself up, swinging one leg over to sit astride him, trying not to let her nervous anticipation show. She should have taken his jeans off first, but there was nothing for it now. She curled her fingers around his tee shirt and lifted.

Immediately his hands slipped around her wrists, locking them in place, twisting them gently away from his tee shirt. He sat up, Thea still across his lap. She felt a stab of apprehension, her eyes flying to his, wanting him to erase her fears. Instead, he refused to meet her gaze.

'Ben?'

He shook his head. She didn't know if he couldn't, or simply wouldn't find the words to explain. She just knew that anger was swiftly replacing the sense of contentment and completeness she'd been feeling only moments earlier.

'What the *hell*, Ben?'

Her eyes were pricking with tears of shame, and she felt utterly vulnerable and exposed. She fought to hold on to the building rage. Anything was better than crying in front of him.

'It's not what you think. Just…leave the shirt, Thea.'

'Leave the tee?' She shook her head, bewildered. And then it dawned. 'The scars?'

He raised his hand to cup her cheek but she batted him away, afraid that the gesture would start the crying. Once she started she didn't think she'd stop.

'We can have sex as long as I don't see your scars?' She could barely see through the tears.

Jackknifing off him, she stood up, grabbing the throw from the couch in a belated attempt at modesty, fervently ignoring the little voice in the back of her head which was trying to remind her that she, too, had her own trust issues. She might be upset with Ben now, but how upset would *he* be if he found out the secret she'd been keeping?

Her arms covered her abdomen, as if protecting the memory.

'I can't do this with you, Ben.' She bounced her head from side to side. 'Not any more. Every time I think we're taking a step forward I let my guard down and you hurt me again.'

'I know, and I'm sorry, Thea.' Ben stood up, buttoning his jeans and reaching to pull her into his arms.

How she dodged him, blinded as she was, she didn't know, but she bolted for the door.

'Please leave, Ben. Not just for tonight. For good. I can't be hurt any more.'

'Thea, just give me time.'

She shook her head. They'd messed up exactly the way she'd feared they would, she thought bitterly.

'I'm sorry, Ben. I've no more time to give you. Please. Just go.'

CHAPTER TEN

BEN WATCHED AS Thea skied down the last section of the run which led off the mountain and down to their private log cabin—practically to their door. His heart thudded as she drew to a stop next to his snowboard, lifted her ski-glasses up and offered him the same wary look she'd been sending his way for the last week.

And he only had himself to blame.

He was grateful that he'd managed to convince her to come here with him. Although he regretted the fact that his convincing had mainly taken the form of admitting that he'd arranged this time off with her colleagues weeks ago, as the honeymoon he and Thea had never had, and reminding her that if she still wanted to keep up the 'happily married' charade she was going to have to come on this so-called holiday after all.

Now he could only try to ensure that he used this as an opportunity to prove to Thea how sorry he really was.

'Good run?' He kept his tone deliberately upbeat.

'Sure.' Her mouth formed the right shape for a smile, but her eyes didn't reflect the sentiment. 'Yours?'

'Yeah. Great.'

His gut twisted every time he thought of that night back at the house and how much he had inadvertently hurt her. *Again*. He'd had no idea that he would suddenly feel so self-conscious about his scars or he would never have initiated such intimacy with Thea in the first instance—however much he'd wanted to. He would never have knowingly put her in a position where she would feel made so completely vulnerable by his actions. But that was exactly what he'd managed to do.

Damn idiot.

He'd gone over and over events in his head, wondering what had prompted that moment of reservation from him, but there was nothing he could put his finger on. He kept picturing Thea's face when he'd emerged from that car with the baby. She had been frightened, angry, relieved—he knew that. But he couldn't shake the sense that there had been something else in her expression…something which didn't fit, which he simply couldn't identify.

He shook his head. *Ridiculous.* And it was wrong of him to try to offload his guilt and his problems onto Thea. He knew what that moment at the crash site had been about. He understood the triggers and the way his mind had shut down. He hadn't seen his surroundings. That burning car might have been an Army Land Rover, the injured passengers his wounded soldiers and the baby an Afghan child, for all he had known at that precise moment.

Thea had been right in her suspicions, so it was hardly any surprise that her face had been such a patchwork of emotions. He was reading too much into it.

'I thought we might eat out tonight,' he suggested casually as Thea flicked her boots out of their ski-clips.

Her wary look cranked up a notch and she narrowed her eyes suspiciously. The casual approach clearly wasn't working.

'I promised you honesty. I think it's time we talked.'

He seemed to be saying that a lot lately. But after decades of stuffing down his emotions perhaps it was only right that he should start to be honest now—with Thea, the person his actions had hurt the most.

She blinked slowly at him, as though she was trying to work out the depth of his sincerity. Then she inclined her head. 'I think you're right.'

The resort staff had been into their cabin and a fresh

basket of fruit sat on the table, a fire roared in the hearth. Thea made her way straight to it, warming her hands and avoiding his gaze.

'Shall we say half an hour?' he suggested.

'No problem.' Her voice was clipped, taut, as she ducked her head and made for her suite on the opposite side of the log cabin to his. Briefly he wondered if she, like him, was fighting to still the questions which swirled around his head.

Now he had finally forced himself to own up to his motivations Ben knew he was never going to be free of his ghosts until he told Thea what had really happened with her brother the day he'd died. She needed to know the truth but he'd never given her that luxury—it had been too hard for him to talk about. But every time he looked at Thea he remembered, and it was this inability to open up—to anyone—which had stopped him from being with Thea.

If he could talk to her about Dan's death he knew he could talk to her about all the ghosts of his past. And that meant he would no longer be emotionally closed off from her. He could be the man she needed him to be. And she could finally, *truly*, be his.

Standing under the jets in the shower in his own suite, Ben tried not to think about Thea in her shower, less than fifteen metres away. Knowing he had acted out of lust, without thinking through any consequences, hadn't stopped him wanting Thea. He could still recall her touch, her taste, her smell, and he felt an aching need for her in the pit of his stomach.

It had taken every ounce of his determination to convince Thea to give him one more chance, to persuade her not to let his moment of uncertainty lead them to discard all the progress they had made in their relationship until that moment. It had come at a cost—he'd finally had to admit to her that there were things he hadn't yet told her—and he'd asked for just a little more time to get his head straight.

Choosing a ski-break—the honeymoon they'd never had—had been his way of proving to her that he really was trying to change. As well as a way of giving them something to talk about and lessening the tension of being around each other—especially when it was just the two of them in their private log cabin, tiptoeing around each other as they had done in the early days at the cottage.

Ben suppressed his frustration. For every two steps forward they seemed to take together it seemed that there was always something to send them a step backwards. But, he rationalised, at least it was *some* kind of progress. However, whilst the choice of location *had* provided a much needed buffer for the last few days, it had perhaps made it *too* easy for them to avoid the real issue, and Ben was determined that tonight they would talk.

By the time she walked back into the living room he was already in the kitchen, downing a pint of water in the hope that it would ease his cracking voice. He turned to face her and instantly his mouth went dry again.

She had left her hair to dry naturally into the loose natural curls he loved. They tumbled around her face and past her shoulders, and even now his fingers itched to slide into their silky depths and pull her lips to his.

A soft, body-hugging lilac cashmere jumper showcased her breasts and slim waist, and tight black jeans curved lovingly over a pert backside which had his body responding like a teenager. The knee-high boots only heightened his reaction—even if they were flat, so that she wouldn't slip in the snow.

What the hell is wrong with you? he berated himself silently. This evening was all about finally telling her what he should have confessed five years ago. Using sex to create an artificial sense of intimacy between them might make him feel better in the short term, but until he could move past that and *really* open up to her they were never going to have a long-term future.

If they could *ever* have a long-term relationship.

Wresting himself from the moment, he strode across the room, snatched up their parkas and, gently throwing hers over her shoulders, opened the door. He ushered her outside to where a horse-drawn sleigh waited patiently outside the cabin. Two inky black horses stood quietly, their breath forming little clouds in the cold air, and Ben heard Thea's nervous intake of breath.

'It's not a big romantic gesture,' he hastily reassured her. 'The restaurant is a couple of valleys over, and this is the best option as it can go cross-country.'

Not entirely a lie. The horse-driven sleigh *was* the most practical way to get to the restaurant. Its long, wide sleigh-skis allowed it to travel easily over the snow-covered countryside, and they could be raised up to allow thick snow-wheels to carry the carriage easily over roads and paths, too. But Ben hadn't been entirely unaware of the romantic connotations and had deliberately chosen it with Thea in mind.

The yellow sleigh was decorated with flowers picked out by gold braiding. Ornate bridles peeked from beneath the blankets which had been temporarily slung over the horses' backs. The lanterns, which adorned the carriage would be lit once night fell.

'Oh.'

Was that good or bad? Ben wondered.

The driver offered them a friendly smile as he jumped down, opening the half-door to the open-topped sleigh and patting the warm rugs which were folded neatly on the seat. Then, moving away, he busied himself with removing the horses' blankets whilst Ben made his way over, offering his hand to Thea as she approached.

He helped her in and swung up afterwards, deliberately sitting on the same side as her, but not too close so as to crowd her. He took the blankets the driver had indicted and opened them up, resisting the urge to brush across Thea and tuck them in. *Another delaying tactic,* he reminded himself, and he wasn't going to create another excuse to put off his confession to another day.

At the driver returned to his seat at the front, and signalled the horses to move off, Ben caught the tilt of Thea's lips. Despite herself, she couldn't help but enjoy the gentle lurching movement and the sound of crunching snow under the horses' hooves and the sleigh's snow-wheels.

This first part of their trip took them around the old town while the driver gave them something of a historical tour of the place. Ben felt Thea relaxing more and more as she engaged with the driver, learning about the area and asking questions. It was so typically *Thea,* Ben was beginning to realise. Although it ruffled him that Thea could be more at ease with a stranger than she was with him right now.

Their tour of the town over, the sleigh made its way out of the central area and towards the lower slopes. The slow, mechanical ratcheting noise of the sleigh-skis coming down was the only sound to punctuate the stillness. The next part of their journey, heading over to a neighbouring town, was about to begin, and as the buildings fell away behind them Ben felt Thea edge forward to talk to the driver about the region itself. Anything to avoid feeling as if she was alone with him, it seemed.

The daunting prospect of their conversation later this evening began to creep up on him, and as Thea learned about the area he leaned back into the soft blankets and listened, distracting his mind.

Finally the sleigh dropped down out of the countryside and into a large, busy town, and soon they stopped outside a non-descript-looking building with heavy, ornate, chunky wooden doors.

Elden Huset—The Firehouse—by name and by former nature.

'We're dining *here*?' Thea glanced up, surprised.

She felt torn. She'd been itching to eat here ever since she'd seen it on a popular cooking show back home. With their 'back to the Stone Age' birchwood fire cooking, the chefs had been lavished with praise, and the whole experience had looked wonderfully sensational. But things with Ben were as awkward as ever, and she couldn't imagine enjoying the experience with such a cloud hanging over them. The sleigh ride had been difficult enough.

He'd told her they were going to talk tonight, but instead of making her feel better it had only made her feel even more on edge. He might not realise it, but Ben wasn't the only one with a confession. She still had to tell him about the baby. *Their* baby. And she didn't relish the thought one little bit.

Allowing Ben to open the door, Thea stepped inside, and the sounds, sights and aromas which instantly assaulted her senses promised her that she was in for an incredible experience.

Despite her initial apprehension, for a while all her concerns receded into the background. With a growing sense of excitement, she moved further inside. The place was all leather, copper and stone, the chefs in flannel shirts, working in an open kitchen where the occasional burst of flame *whooshed* up towards the thick, oak-timber-beamed ceilings in a blaze of glory which ignited her sense of smell and her tastebuds with tantalising delight.

'This place is incredible...' She inhaled the smoky scent with deep, appreciative breaths, hearing the sound of crackling birchwood and clanging copper pots, which lent an exciting edge to the atmosphere.

Thea's eyes were drawn to the smooth grace of the chefs, working in such harmony, and she watched as one chef took a generous piece of salmon, wrapped it in hay, and thrust it onto the bars above the fire. The flames took hold of the hay and the fire blazed over the salmon in seconds, leaving it apparently black and burned-looking. Then the chef turned it over to repeat the action, before taking the fillet out and sliding it onto another tray, which he slid into what looked like a wood furnace.

Remembering Ben, she turned—only to find he was also watching the proceedings with the same look of intensity on his face that she'd had. Somehow it helped her to relax a little, and she was able to enjoy watching the chef pulling the tray out of the oven. In one slick, efficient movement he peeled the blackened skin off the salmon to reveal a pink, perfectly cooked piece of fish. Her mouth practically watered even as he finished serving it up, and she swallowed once…twice.

'I'm having *that*,' she declared, as soon as she'd regained control of her mouth.

The spectacle of the restaurant had changed the atmosphere between them—if only temporarily. And by the time they'd ordered and their meal had arrived Thea was beginning to feel comfortable enough to just enjoy this part of the evening without being wrapped up in what happened next.

'My mum used to love to cook,' Ben said suddenly—unexpectedly.

She opened her mouth, then closed it again. When he had promised her they would talk tonight, this wasn't what she had expected. Ben had *never* talked about his family—not to her, at least. She'd gleaned from Daniel, before she'd ever met Ben, that Ben's mother had died when he was young—maybe the same age Thea had been when her own parents had been killed.

'It must have been hard for you when she died.' She knew exactly what he must have gone through. 'Isn't your father in the Army, like you?'

'Yes, he's in the Army—but he's not medical, like me.' Ben answered her question, then reflected for a moment before continuing. 'And you're right—it wasn't easy. Although it must have been worse for you, losing *both* your parents. After Mum's death my father cleared out all reminders of her from the house. Photos, jewellery—*anything* she had loved and valued. We never spoke about her again.'

'Never?' Thea replied, shocked. It was so different from the way Daniel had helped her when their own parents had died. He'd made a scrapbook of photos and memories, so that she'd felt she would never forget them. He'd talked to her as often as she had wanted, answered as many questions as she'd asked, and almost always found some way to make her laugh again.

Her brother's endless support and love had nurtured her spirit, influencing her to become the person she was today. She couldn't imagine how it would have affected her to have been forbidden from talking about her parents. If Ben had been almost *conditioned* not to think talk about his mother from a child, was it any wonder that he found it so difficult to open up to her...to *anyone*...now? He and Daniel had been close, but she was beginning to understand why Ben was so closed off.

'What else do you remember about your mum?' Thea asked tentatively.

'Plenty.' His voice was thick, loaded. 'My father might have taken everything tangible of hers which I wanted to cherish—photos of her, the emerald necklace I always remembered her wearing, even the damned sofa cushions she loved to sew—but he couldn't take my memories.'

Couldn't take my memories...

The words punched through to her stomach. How many times had she thought the same thing about her baby? She might have lost the one thing she had cherished the most, but the love was still there, the memory of that feeling of knowing a life was growing inside her. That single scan.

'She used to teach me how to bake cakes as a kid,' Ben continued hesitantly, as though he was fighting to speak. 'Then how to cook.'

'Is that where you learned to make the pancakes you cooked me that time?' Curiosity crept over her.

'Yes—and thanks to her I can rustle up something a bit better if I want to. I can even make a mean Madagascan vanilla bean soufflé. I once dreamed of becoming a chef when I grew up.'

'Really? What did your mum think?'

Ben hunched his shoulders. 'She encouraged it. She never wanted me to become a soldier—she was frightened she'd lose me. I've always wondered, if I hadn't gone into the Army, if I might have made it as a chef. I'd have loved to start something like this. It's right up my street.'

'I can see you as a chef...' Thea murmured. 'Why didn't you do it? Too many memories?'

'No. My father didn't encourage it, and I always wanted to please him so I followed his lead.'

'And *did* it please him?' she couldn't help asking.

Ben pulled a face. 'There was never *any* pleasing him. But I didn't find that out until much later on, and by then I'd already chosen my path. So I made it work for me and decided to have nothing more to do with him.'

Thea stayed quiet. She missed her family. They weren't around to talk to and she'd have given anything for one last conversation. It was unimaginable to her that Ben should be in a position where he *could* talk to his father, but that things were so bad he didn't want to.

Her heart suddenly ached for him. His relationship with his father wasn't something she'd ever thought about, but now she couldn't stop wondering what kind of a father Ben would have made himself. Even given the circumstances, somehow she didn't think he would have abandoned her—or his baby. Or put them through whatever *he* had been through.

The guilt pressed in on her with even more force.

'Would you ever leave the Army and try?' she asked, trying to jog the thought from her head.

'What? Becoming a chef? No chance. Too old now!' Ben laughed.

'You love being a Major?' She struggled to keep her tone light, to betray none of the sadness she felt for him. Or her self-reproach.

A shadow crossed his face. 'Not any more. I've worked hard, I've done my duty, I've given my all. But now I don't think I have any more to give.'

'But you would never *leave*?' She held her breath in shock.

'I'd like to, but… I still feel tied in. I'm working on it.'

Thea knew she was staring. Hastily she averted her gaze, but her mind was swimming. She'd thought the Army was his life—she'd never thought he would consider leaving.

Ben moved his hand across the table to take hers, turning it over gently and rubbing his thumb on her palm.

'I'm sorry.' He looked her straight in the eyes. 'About the other night.'

Was it only such a short while ago? It almost felt a lifetime earlier.

'It should never have happened.'

She could only stare at him. It was happening again—*another mistake.* She was such an idiot.

But he was pressing on uncomfortably. 'After that motorway call-out I finally admitted to myself I still had feelings for you—I was driven by some need for you. I should have controlled it—waited until I'd addressed the issues which had kept us apart in the first place. I hope I haven't ruined it between us.'

'So you still…want me?' Her mind was reeling.

'Yes. And I'm sorry for not trusting you, Thea, for not wanting you to see my scars. You've only ever been supportive and that was unfair of me and so very wrong.'

'*Why* didn't you trust me?' Thea asked quietly, still trying absorb the fact that he wasn't rejecting her. *Again.*

'I don't know. I know that you'll be there for me, no matter what. You've already proved that. There's no one single thing I can pinpoint. But I guess the day before had been a traumatic day for everyone, and I don't find it easy to talk anyway. With memories of my own accident, it all came to a head. And maybe I felt as though you were holding back a little.'

'Do you really believe that?' Thea's heart lurched with guilt. 'That I was holding back?'

'I don't know.' Ben shook his head apologetically. 'No. Probably not. I was trying to deflect. You were right. I wasn't exactly thinking straight during that RTC. Anyway, I'm sorry.'

'Don't be.' Thea swallowed. After seeing him save that baby her head had been all over the place—it was no wonder Ben had picked up on that.

'No. I am sorry. I should have trusted you enough to tell you. I didn't, and that wasn't right. You deserve better than that from me.'

Thea felt her eyes prick—couldn't look up from the remnants of her meal. He thought she deserved better but he was right—she *had* been holding back. She was *still* holding back. Ever since he'd walked towards her with that baby she'd been fighting to shut out the painful memories. And Ben was a part of them. With every new confession he made to her it only made her feel more conscience-stricken. It was time to tell him the truth. Because—really—didn't *he* deserve better from *her*?

'Thea? Are you all right?'

His evident concern only heightened her gnawing guilt. She pushed her chair back and rose to her feet. Words were lodged in her throat and she had to force them out.

'Can we get out of here?'

He frowned. She didn't blame him for being confused. Still, he nodded and stood up too.

'I'll find someone and pay.' He glanced around for a waiter, signalled to him, then turned back.

She couldn't bear the way he was looking at her.

'I'll wait outside,' she muttered, turning swiftly and doing all she could not to run for the door.

The cold night air made her bury her head in her jumper. In her haste she'd forgotten her coat, and it was freezing out here. She stopped, half turning back to the restaurant, knowing she would have to go in but unable to bring herself to do so. No—better to find their sleigh and grab one of the blankets from there.

Before she could go any further the door to the restaurant opened and Ben appeared. He jogged over to her, wrapping her in her coat so solicitously that she batted away his hands before tears overwhelmed her.

'Don't, Ben, please. I don't deserve your kindness.'

'You're wrong.'

His certainty only made her feel worse.

'Please—just let me say this.'

He hesitated for a long moment before taking a reluctant step backwards, as if to give her space. Oddly, it made her feel alone. She stared down at the slush-covered cobbles, unable to meet his eye. Then, somewhere deep inside herself, she found the edge of her forgotten resolve and dragged her gaze up to his. She owed him that.

'The night we… Our wedding night,' she corrected hastily. 'Oh…there's no easy way to say this. There was a baby. *Our* baby.'

CHAPTER ELEVEN

BEN STARED AT her for several long moments.

Their baby?

His chest started to constrict acutely. *Where was she... he...? Why hadn't Thea told him before?*

His head fought to catch up with the words she'd used. 'There *was* a baby?' he asked urgently.

Thea nodded, and her head bounced madly around as though it wasn't even her own, as if it had been let loose on some kind of out-of-control spring.

'You...terminated?'

The words made him feel nauseous, even though his head, trying frantically to keep up with his racing heart, was desperately trying to caution him. He was in no place to judge Thea, or to censure her. But why hadn't she told him? He could have supported her, made sure she knew all her options before making that momentous decision.

'No!' She jerked her head up.

Everything seemed to stop for him.

No? No, what?

'But you didn't have it?'

He heard the catch in his voice, berated himself for it. But he was powerless against it.

The look she darted at him was evidence that Thea was frenziedly trying to work out what he was thinking. He opened his mouth but no words came out.

'I lost it.' She stopped abruptly. That just made it seem as if she'd been careless. She cleared her throat and met his eye again. 'I miscarried.'

Her voice cracked but her emotion, the look in her eyes, told him all the things she couldn't say.

'When?' he asked, struggling to keep his voice from betraying any emotion for fear of upsetting her further. Inside he was in turmoil. 'How far along were you?'

'Three months. It was ten days after the first scan. I... I started to bleed.'

'Were you...okay?' It wasn't what he meant, but she seemed to understand anyway.

She squeezed her eyes shut.

'It's been five years, but even now, remembering that day, I can still recall exactly how I felt in that instant. Blind fear and...and...utter sorrow. There's no way to properly articulate that.'

He should have known—should have been there for her.

'I'm sorry. I'm so, so sorry,' he whispered, but he didn't think she was even hearing him. 'Time heals,' he offered helplessly, but it sounded hollow to his ears. It hadn't healed the loss of his own mother, and it hadn't with the loss of Dan. Or was that his own guilt?

Thea shook her head, swallowing hard.

'I'm not so sure about that. With my parents, with Daniel, certainly the edges have dulled. Slightly. Given enough time. But the pain has never gone away completely.'

Ben nodded. He knew that feeling well.

'But with a baby it's different, somehow. Every year I think about what could have been. Every year, when I see a child the same age as...as ours would have been, I imagine whether it would have been crawling, walking, talking, playing, jumping, laughing.'

A sob suddenly escaped from somewhere deep inside her, tearing at Ben's gut.

'I can't even say *he* or *she*. I have to say *it*.' She looked up at him with an expression of pure anguish as she asked helplessly, 'Does that make it better or worse?'

He shook his head, unable to speak. Reaching out, he

placed his hands on her shoulders and pulled her, ignoring her resistance, until she was in his arms. Rigid. Unyielding. But there, none the less.

'It doesn't make it anything,' he whispered hoarsely. 'It just *is*.'

They stood like that for a few moments, Thea still stiff in his embrace, before she pushed herself out of his hold, crossing her arms in front of her chest protectively.

He wanted to stop her…wanted to offer her more support, more relief—*more*. His head felt as if it was too small for his swirling emotions.

He took a step back. 'You never called me. You should have called.' He hadn't intended for it to sound like an accusation.

She squeezed her eyes shut, willing herself to keep control.

'To say what?' she asked flatly.

'To *tell* me about it. To say you needed me, that you weren't okay—*anything*.'

He practically shouted the last word and Thea winced as people in the street turned in their direction.

'Thea, I didn't mean that—sorry.' He raked his hand through his hair as he turned in a circle. Then turned to face her square-on. Her eyes were filled with torment.

'You should have called me, Thea. I would have come back in a heartbeat.'

'What would have been the point?' She hunched her shoulders. 'We weren't together. You'd walked out on me.'

'I didn't abandon you,' he hissed. 'We've been through this. You *told* me to leave.'

Why were they attacking each other? He needed to end this. *Now*.

'I take that back unreservedly,' he said immediately. 'We've been through that already. But, Thea, you still should have called me.'

'And said what? That I *had been* pregnant, but not to worry because I'd lost it?'

'Thea…' he growled in warning. 'You should have called me before then. The moment you knew you were pregnant. You should have called me *then*.'

'You were…busy,' she muttered weakly.

He felt the brush of disgust. 'You're better than that, Thea.'

She glared at him, then drew in a deep breath.

'I'm sorry. Maybe you're right. Maybe I should have called as soon as I knew. But I *thought* you'd walked out on me—I believed you didn't want anything to do with me—and I didn't see the point in involving you in something you wouldn't want to be a part of. Or at least something I *thought* you wouldn't want to be a part of.'

He stared at her in disbelief. Realisation dawned.

'Wait. You thought I wouldn't want it? That I'd suggest you terminate it?'

He felt physically sick.

'I didn't know!' she cried, spreading her hands helplessly. Then she stopped to fix him with her direct gaze. Her voice was calmer, firm. 'I just didn't know, Ben. You *must* see that.'

He felt as if he'd just been punched in the solar plexus and was struggling to draw breath. Was that really how she felt about him?

'I see.'

They both stood, motionless. Neither quite sure where to go or what to do.

He wanted to say more.

There was nothing left *to* say.

Ben turned around, looking for the sleigh. If the journey over here had been strained, the return leg was going to be excruciating. But there was nothing else for it.

His arm felt like a ten-ton weight as he signalled the driver and marched over. Thea followed behind, reluctance emanating from her with every step. As before, he offered her his hand, but unlike before she took it awkwardly, trying to maintain as little contact as possible while still accepting his help with cold politeness. He practically vaulted up into the sleigh behind her, watching her scoot as far away from him as possible, and tugging a blanket up around her neck, her face turned away.

Even in the moonlight her profile looked so full of misery that he was hit with remorse. This evening was supposed to have been about him opening up to her. Now his head was roiling and tumbling and he was unable to work out how he felt, let alone comfort Thea. He knew he was angry. He just didn't know at whom or about what.

He had a feeling it was himself.

Thea stared at the ceiling. The bed was a jumbled mess from where she'd been tossing and turning for the last five hours.

Tonight had been absolute purgatory. She'd expected it would be—that was exactly why she had dreaded telling him, had put it off again and again. However, she had never once imagined that it would be such a nightmare because he would feel so hurt. She had expected panic, anger, relief. She had never considered devastation, anger, loss.

Now that she was beginning to come down from the peak of her rampaging emotions she wasn't sure what to make of it. Turning over to her right side and then back to her left proved no more satisfactory. Sleep wasn't to be her friend tonight. She threw off the covers and grabbed her fleece jacket, hoping that she could resurrect something of the fire from its smouldering embers, and padded out into the living room.

She saw that Ben was staring into the flames of a roaring fire the moment she walked through the door. She froze, but it was too late.

'Can't sleep either,' he murmured. 'I've just made coffee. Do you want one?'

'Please.' She matched his tone, grateful that they didn't appear to be about to start arguing again.

She sat on the other couch, the warmth of the fire seeping into her bones and making her feel better—if only a little bit. Then Ben was back with her coffee.

'I'm sorry. Maybe I should have told you...'

'I'm sorry. I shouldn't have reacted like that...'

They both spoke, and stopped, in unison.

Thea flushed. 'Go ahead.'

'I'm sorry, I shouldn't have reacted that way,' Ben apologised. 'Just the idea of you not telling me, going through it alone—whichever way it played out... Either an absentee father, or a man who leaves the woman he got pregnant to deal with everything alone—that isn't the man I would ever have chosen to be. And then to think of what you had to go through... It just isn't the person I want to think of myself as.'

There was no doubting the sincerity of his words, and Thea nodded awkwardly.

The silence was slightly less taut than it had been before and they sat sipping their coffee as logs crackled in the fire. Thea even unzipped her fleece quietly.

'I have a picture,' she said suddenly. 'A scan.'

Ben's head snapped up. 'Of our baby?'

Our baby. She'd never expected to hear those words drop so easily from his lips. She nodded, ducking into her room to fish her purse out of her bag. She almost hesitated by the door, but then she drew together whatever courage she could and propelled herself forward.

Ben took the scan picture without a sound. His eyes never left the black and white image, and his finger almost imperceptibly twitched, as if to stroke the tiny peanut shape.

'You can keep it. If you like,' she offered tentatively. 'I have another.'

He nodded, slipped his wallet out of his pocket and slid the image inside.

But as he went to close it Thea's hand stayed the movement. A single photo had caught her attention.

'May I?'

He looked as though he was going to object, then abruptly handed the wallet to her. She turned the image towards her, her heart thudding. The man in the photo was younger than he'd looked on the two occasions she'd seen him observing Ben's recovery in the hospital, but it was definitely him—the man she'd assumed was some kind of psychiatrist or counsellor. But what would *that* man be doing in this old photo, with his arm around Ben, and next to them Daniel, looking proud. She peered closer at the man's rank.

'This is the Colonel who commanded you and Daniel?'

Ben stayed silent.

She was pretty sure the answer was obvious but she needed to hear it. 'Ben?' she pushed.

'Yes, that's the Colonel when he was younger,' Ben said eventually. 'And, yes, to what you're thinking. He's also my father.'

That wasn't what she'd been thinking, and now the wheels were spinning in her head as she tried to catch up. So this was Ben's father—the same man who had commanded Ben and Daniel, and of whom Daniel had always thought so highly. The father Ben had cut out of his life on any personal basis. And yet he still kept this photograph in his wallet.

'Have you ever thought about talking to him?' she offered tentatively. 'About what happened? How you feel?'

Ben snorted. 'About Dan's death? Me getting blown up? No. He wouldn't care. His only priority is for me to get on with my recovery and get on with the next mission.'

'His only priority? How can he not care? You work together every day.'

'It's not like that. You don't understand.'

Ben sighed, as though the whole topic of his father was too tedious for discussion.

'When I say he's my Commander, you think we work together in the field hospital like some cosy father-and-son duo. We don't—we never have. I'm a trauma surgeon—one of around two hundred medics out there, with a Lieutenant Colonel as my direct Officer in Command. My father is a full Colonel—IC of the whole battalion, with up to four thousand men under his command. My unit of two hundred is a drop in the ocean. Granted, we might cross paths occasionally out there, but he would never go out of his way to talk to me. He probably wouldn't even know if we were at the same base. The last time I saw him was about a month before my accident. He was holding a command briefing for the Lieutenant Colonels on our camp and he conducted a quick check of my field hospital with my Commanding Officer. But we barely saw each other, let alone exchanged pleasantries.'

It would seem for all the world as though he didn't care. Only Thea knew Ben did care, deep down, whether he realised it or not.

Thea thought back to the times when she'd seen his father in the hospital when Ben had first been brought home. 'And what about him coming back here?'

'And leave his command to someone else? He wouldn't consider it for a moment,' Ben refuted flatly, then added dismissively. 'Even if he wanted to he couldn't.'

She wavered. *Ben needed to know. He carried a photo of the man in his wallet.*

She licked her lips. 'You do know he was at the hospital, don't you?'

Ben jerked his head up. The look of hope that flashed

through his eyes, if only for a fraction of a second, was heartbreaking.

'When?' Ben peered at her, then shook his head. 'No. I told you—he was in Afghanistan. He wouldn't have returned.'

'He did,' Thea insisted. 'I saw him several times outside your room when you were first flown back, consulting with your doctors. They definitely seemed to be deferring to him. The other time was in the gardens, the day you decided to take your souped-up wheelchair for a test drive into the hospital bushes.'

'You've got the wrong man,' Ben said flatly.

'No. I haven't.' This was harder than she'd thought, but she couldn't let up now. 'He's older now, of course, and his hair is grey, but the cut is still the same and the face is clearly his.'

Ben shook his head.

She needed one last jolt.

'He was definitely the Colonel from the photograph in your wallet.' She steeled herself for the next bit. 'The one with Daniel.'

Even then Ben refused to believe her. Drained, she had no choice but to let it go, and when he changed the subject she let him. But the very fact he'd told her who the man was gave Thea even more hope.

'Anyway, thanks for the scan pic,' he muttered, finally slipping his wallet into his back pocket.

'Sure,' she managed awkwardly, sipping her coffee again and watching the flames lick over the logs.

'Would you have told me?' Ben asked suddenly. 'In the end? If you *had* had the baby? Earlier? I mean, say, four years ago?'

She'd often wondered about that. The answer had always been the same. 'Probably.'

'You think so?'

She nodded. 'I think probably just before I was due. I

couldn't have imagined the baby being born and not giving you the chance to be there. I still... I still loved you back then. And I couldn't have faced my child in the future and told it I hadn't been able to put aside my own pride to give it a chance a relationship with you.'

He stared into the fire again, then said simply, 'Thank you.'

It was odd. His entire reaction to the news of their baby had been unexpected. For the first time Thea didn't feel quite so alone. But she still felt raw, exposed, and she knew Ben's revelations about his father had left him feeling equally vulnerable.

Tentatively they began to make small talk, but she wasn't really surprised when Ben suddenly leaned forward and took her face in her hands, then kissed her.

The kiss conveyed all the raw emotion that had been circling around them all evening. Tonight the flimsy veil had been lifted on the void which was always inside her, and his deep, searching, almost fervent kiss let her know he was feeling just as vulnerable and exposed.

His kiss was almost desperate, and it mirrored every fear and emotion in her gut. She responded to it on a primal level, allowing Ben to pull her to her feet so that they could get closer, and his hands moved quickly over her back, around to her front, grazing her breast through the fabric.

She wanted to let him carry on, take more from her, give her more. But she couldn't—not yet. She stilled his hand uncertainly. As much as her body was crying out for them to make love, to give that empty feeling some relief, if only temporarily, her mind couldn't quite let go of the last time. She didn't want that rejection again.

Suddenly Ben pulled back from her, leaving her feeling momentarily bereft, before she realised he had lifted his jumper and tee over his head in one movement and now stood, unmoving and wordless, in front of her. Slowly she took in the long, thin scars which circled his arm, from where it had been reattached, the thick, circular splodge of a scar under his armpit, from where the surgeons had entered his chest cavity, and the criss-cross of scars over various parts of his torso from where metal debris and bullets had grazed his skin. Silvery and light in some places and angry red welts in others.

Her raw sadness was dulled slightly, somewhat eased by the enormity of the step Ben had taken in letting her see them. She took them all in, her eyes raking from one to another to another and back. Finally she took a step forward, reaching a tentative hand out to touch them, half expecting him to pull away, surprised when her fingers ran softly over his skin and still he didn't reject her. But his body was taut, his apprehension spilling out in his body language, and Thea longed to set him at ease.

Dipping her head down, she only hesitated for a fraction of a second before letting her lips make contact with the damaged skin. She dropped little kisses at first, becoming bolder when he remained motionless, his hands clenched by his sides as if he was fighting an internal battle. She trailed kisses down the criss-crosses, lower and lower, until they dipped out of sight beneath the waistband of his jeans.

She leaned back to look at him in silent question. Was he ready to trust her completely?

His hands moved to unbutton the jeans, stilling as she covered them with her own, her eyes never leaving his as she stripped him of the rest of his clothing. Finally he was standing naked and proud in front of her, the trust she had wanted at last in evidence. As well as something more.

Sensing her ultimate capitulation, Ben pulled Thea to him and swept her into his arms as he lowered them both quickly to the rug. Despite herself, Thea knew that tonight was about losing themselves in each other. Masking the grief they were both feeling. In some ways she could see Ben's actions as progress. But what was driving them might be a step forward, or it might be another scurry backwards.

CHAPTER TWELVE

BEN CONCENTRATED ON the slope, acutely aware of Thea skiing so close next to him, acutely aware of *everything* she was dong. After last night things should have been good between them. Better than good. He had finally trusted her enough to let her see his scars—the unmistakable evidence that he'd survived a war which had indiscriminately taken the lives of others. Taken the life of Dan.

But showing Thea those scars was only part of it. He bore other scars. Scars which couldn't be seen. Emotional scars from the bomb blast, from Dan's death, and until he let Thea see those—as incredible as the sex had been between them—there was no shaking the truth that things had happened out of sequence. As a result of raw emotions. And they both knew that.

Thea's revelation about their baby had sent him reeling. Last night it had been an incredible shock. But in the cold light of day the shock was receding and he felt as though a hollow emptiness was tearing a hole inside him. How could you miss something, feel such pain and loss, for a baby you had never even known about? And yet he felt as though he was grieving that, too.

Somehow Thea's secret had given him the excuse of avoiding telling her about Dan—yet again. But he knew that until that final obstacle was removed, once and for all, there could be no future for them.

He hurtled around a bend, lost in his thoughts, until a movement in the next valley caught his eye.

'Are you trying to kill us?'

Thea almost skidded into a snowbank as she edged her skis hard into the ice to avoid a collision. Breathing hard from her exertions, she made her way up to him, her voice loaded with shock.

'Look over there,' he instructed, ignoring her fury. Then, as she failed to react to his order, he moved to stand behind her, lining up her eyes with his arm. 'Across the valley.'

It didn't take her long to realise what he was trying to show her.

'An avalanche.' She sucked in a breath. 'And a skier? What's he even doing there?'

'From the bright yellow jacket, I'd hazard a guess he's Mountain Patrol, checking the slopes. He'll probably be okay.'

'Right…' Thea nodded, watching the skilled skier racing down the piste, trying to outrun the avalanche. There was a gap in the treeline to the side of the piste, which he was clearly aiming for, and Thea watched as the patroller reached the gap and practically did a one-eighty turn on his pole to drop back on himself, off the piste and onto the narrow, tree-free path twenty feet below, just as the avalanche thundered by above.

She exhaled a *whoosh* of relief, but even as she did so the skier either caught a hidden rock or slid on the ice. He had fallen, and was now hurtling down the slope on his stomach, his skis flying into the air with frightening sprays of snow.

'He's not going to be able to stop himself!' cried Thea as the skier headed straight towards a wooded embankment.

Sixty feet into the slide, the skier slammed straight into a tree—head-first.

Time stopped for Ben, and it was as if his surroundings spun around him. Snow, desert, skis, tanks, bodies. He ripped his snowboard off and threw it into the webbing on his back. Through the fug in his head he vaguely heard Thea scream at him, but her words were indistinguishable.

Something about a death wish. At some point she might have grabbed his arm, but he threw her off without a glance and then he was jumping down the steep embankment, letting himself fall and fall into the valley, hoping he'd land on soft snow and not hard rocks.

Wading through thigh-deep snow, he felt his back screaming at him, already on fire, but he ignored the pain and pushed on towards the immobile body. His mind kept switching the figure of the skier on the snowy slopes for Dan, bleeding out on the rocky mountainside. There was no way he could leave him there.

He had no idea how long the interminable trek across the valley took. The relief when he finally reach the skier and saw the man had his eyes open was indescribable. The guy was alive. Even better, the man's eyes widened slightly upon seeing him. A trickle of relief crept down Ben's spine. At least it meant the man still had some cognitive function.

'Don't try to nod or shake your head. Try not to move at all for the moment. If you can't talk, just blink.'

'I can talk,' the man rasped, clearly having trouble breathing.

'Okay, that's good. I was on the run down the mountain to the village and I saw everything. I'm Ben, by the way. Can you remember what happened to you?'

'Ben…okay. I'm Tomas. I was patrolling the unmarked slopes, looking for any extreme skiers. I triggered a snow slide and I was trying to outrun it. I thought I dropped down safely…but maybe I fell? I don't recall much after that.'

'Good—that's good.' Ben nodded encouragingly. 'Can you move your arms and legs?'

'I don't know.' Tomas was clearly having trouble concentrating. 'Are you a doctor?'

'A trauma surgeon.' Ben nodded again.

'Both of you?'

Ben froze as Tomas's gaze lifted to just over his right shoulder. He turned slowly but he already knew what he was going to find. Thea, white-faced but resolute, stood behind him. His stomach slid away in fear. She'd only come because of *him*. If she got hurt it would be *his* fault.

He moved away so Tomas wouldn't hear him.

'Are you crazy?' he hissed. 'You could have killed yourself.'

'No more than you could have,' she countered angrily. 'You shouldn't have come over here. You *know* the snow is probably unstable. There was a heavy snowfall last night, and it must have landed on a layer of compact ice. The whole lot is probably ready to slide at any moment. You could be just the provocation it needs.'

Fear clawed at him. 'Dammit, Thea, if anything happens to you I'll never forgive myself.'

'Then you'd better hope nothing does happen to me.' Thea jutted her chin out determinedly, but inside she was shaking. 'I couldn't just leave you to it, Ben. Odds are it'll need two of us to stabilise him. Then I'll ski down to the town.'

'You need to get out of here,' he argued in desperation. 'You know how time-critical this is.'

'It's only time-critical if there's a stable patient,' countered Thea. 'It wouldn't matter how fast I got down there if you can't stabilise him. He wouldn't live long enough for rescue to arrive.'

She had a point. Ben shook his head, hardly daring to say another word.

Sensing she was gaining ground, Thea pushed her point home. 'We're the eyes and ears for the local trauma unit. The more information we can gather and pass on, the more pinpointed their subsequent care can be.'

His glower raked over her. He looked exhausted and scared.

'You've got some nerve…' His voice shook but he said nothing more.

He turned back to the skier.

'Tomas, our priority right now is to get you comfortable while we assess your injuries.'

Tomas fought to draw a deep breath. 'I was sliding, and then I remember a hot, searing pain travelling from my head to my toes.'

'Yeah,' Ben confirmed. 'You hit a tree—good job you were wearing a helmet. So, have you got your patrol two-way radio?'

'Should be in my pocket... If you call in, they can send another patroller with a toboggan. Then they can take me to a landing zone a bit further down, where a chopper can land to medevac me.'

Ben checked Tomas's pockets, then looked at Thea. The radio had been lost in the slide.

'Tomas did have a toboggan though,' Thea murmured quietly.

'Understood.' Ben nodded. 'Okay, Tomas, I'm just going to pinch your thigh—you tell me if you can feel it.'

'No...' He closed his eyes for a moment. 'But I think I can move my hands.'

Ben watched carefully as only two fingers on one of Tomas's hands twitched. Thea cast him a sinking look, they needed to stabilise Tomas fast and go for help.

Thea kept her voice deliberately neutral, clearly not wanting to lie to the man but needing to offer some re-assurance. 'There is *some* visible movement—try not to worry. I'm just going to prep you for when they arrive with the full transport.'

She had barely finished speaking when Tomas went into cardiac arrest.

Uttering low curses, they started chest compressions, relieved when Tomas came back relatively quickly.

'Wait, there's his rucksack,' Thea spied suddenly. She waded through the snow and retrieved a small pouch, open-ing it... 'Space blanket, water camel, emergency medical kit—that's something.'

Before Ben could answer Tomas went into cardiac arrest again, and with barely a glance between them they resumed their places to work together. It took longer this time, and the look Thea cast him confirmed Ben's apprehension.

They made Tomas comfortable before carefully retreating a small distance.

'He won't cope with continually going into cardiac arrest,' Ben murmured. 'I'm pretty sure it's the paralysis which is causing the problem. I think it's causing his diaphragm to stop rising and falling and that's what's knocking his heart out.'

'That makes sense.' Thea nodded. 'But there's nothing here to help him breathe in the interim, is there?'

Ben paused. 'Maybe…'

She followed his eyes to the water camel.

'It's not ideally sterile, but the long tube could be put into cold snow to harden it slightly.'

Thea grunted, not keen. 'Might be hard to intubate without a sedative but he will need to be stable enough for me to go for help.'

'Then there's nothing else for it,' Ben confirmed. 'If Tomas goes into cardiac arrest a third time we'll use the opportunity to intubate before starting compressions.'

'And then?'

'If we can't get Mountain Rescue to Tomas, we'll just have to get Tomas to them,' Ben ground out.

'How?'

'Find his rescue toboggan. He had it right up until the last moment. It can't be far away.'

It was a long shot, but they both searched the landscape in silence.

'Over there,' Thea cried out.

Ben swung around, following the direction of her outstretched arm. The toboggan wasn't too far away, but the slope wasn't a used one and the snow didn't look bedded in.

'Don't move,' he commanded as Thea edged her skis

towards the slope, preparing to ski up the mountain. 'I'll go. You stay here with Tomas.'

Thea shook her head. 'I have skis. I can side-slip up there. If I feel the snow start to give, I can ski out of there before the slide starts. You only have a snowboard—you can't do it the same way.'

'Makes no difference.' He shook his head.

She snorted, half-angry, half-frustrated. 'Of *course* it makes a difference. What makes your life any less valuable than mine? No—don't answer that. Like you said, this whole thing is time-critical. I need to go, and you need to get back to Tomas in case he arrests again.'

Before Ben could say anything else she was off, carefully edging up the mountain, step by step, until she could traverse across to the toboggan. She knew he wanted to stop her, wanted to send her for help, but he also had to know that she was right. If they wanted to save Tomas and give the man any chance at a halfway decent recovery then they needed to get that toboggan.

He stood and watched her for several moments, inching very carefully up the treacherous slope, her heart in her mouth. She was relieved when his focus had to be split between the man lying on the snow in front of him and her, as she inched her way further and further into danger. She knew he'd be worried that she was too far away for him to do anything about it if something went wrong. This was exactly why he hadn't wanted her here. It was also exactly why *she* hadn't wanted *him* here. But he hadn't listened to her. She didn't think he'd even registered her.

Her heart hammering, she reached the toboggan and dug its metal arms out of the snow. Then, pulling it behind her, she skied carefully back down to Ben and Tomas. Ben practically snatched the handles out of her hands.

'How is he?' She kept her voice low.

'Slipping in and out of consciousness,' Ben murmured. 'We need to get him down.'

'Right.' She checked the rucksack she'd recovered. 'We can stabilise his neck, then get the scoop around him.'

Working quickly and carefully, they manoeuvred Tomas into position. He was barely conscious, and they could feel time slipping through their fingers.

'You need to ski into town now,' he told her when they were finished. 'Be sure to stay well ahead of us in case the toboggan dislodges anything and it rolls down to you. Thea, remember this isn't a designated slope—it isn't safe. Be careful.'

She frowned. 'Wait—you're on foot?'

Ben shrugged, and she realised that of course it wasn't as though he could pull the toboggan on his snowboard. Quickly releasing herself from her skis, she circled around him to grab his board from the webbing he'd thrown on to the snow earlier.

'I'll take the snowboard—you take my skis.'

'You can't snowboard,' Ben objected irritably.

'No—I don't *enjoy* it as much as skiing. Doesn't mean I *can't*. I'll get down faster than if I'm trying to ski through the snow anyway. And there's no way you can walk and pull a toboggan.'

'That's an impossible maze of trees and rocks to try to navigate,' he argued.

'And I won't be trying to do it whilst pulling a seriously injured man on a scoop.'

He closed his eyes for a moment. 'I just want you off this dangerous slope. I want you safe. I don't want an argument keeping you on this damned mountain any longer.'

'So put on the skis and do what I'm suggesting.' She stood her ground.

'Fine.' He gritted his teeth. 'Thanks.'

She flipped the board around, clipped her ski boots in, and started off slowly down the wooded, rock-littered slope, trying to quell the rising terror. How was Ben possibly going to navigate it without causing more injury to Tomas? Alone, with only his ghosts to keep him company?

All along he had refused to entertain the idea of losing the skier. It meant more to him than just the rescue that it was. She'd seen the haunted look that had veiled his eyes the moment he'd seen the skier lying prone on the snow. Another of those PTSD triggers...

Thea wondered if he would ever be able to open up to her about that darkness he carried with him. She wanted to help him, but she wasn't sure she could. Not until he wanted to help himself. She had a feeling that unless he did there was no hope of a future for them together.

Tonight she was going to push him. Tonight would be his final chance to let her in.

Lost in her thoughts, she was down the mountain safely before she realised it. She raced to the Mountain Rescue centre and alerted the team. Then, explaining she was a trauma doctor, she convinced them to let her on the helicopter to show them where she and Ben had agreed their Emergency Rendezvous point would be.

Finally, she spotted him, painstakingly picking his way through the trees, near to the lower treeline and close to where the helicopter was now landing. Ben approached them smoothly, quickly, his body betraying nothing of his own pain. But Thea knew his body had been pushed too far today. However there was no disguising his fury at her return as she jumped down from the chopper.

'Your wife briefed us,' the rescue team leader acknowledged, taking the scoop from Ben and prepping Tomas for the flight.

'Good.' Ben nodded. 'Tomas went into cardiac arrest a third time. I had to improvise, using a water camel as a breathing tube. I'd recommend administering a sedative for the flight, and using a bag valve mask to force air into his lungs.'

Accepting the team's hurried gratitude, Ben and Thea

moved out of the way as the helicopter took off, the snow around them swirling in a mass of chaos. Then the chopper flew away and the snow dropped down silently, deadly, as an equally heavy silence shrouded the two of them.

Wordlessly they exchanged skis and snowboard. Thea felt exhausted. The rescue had been draining and all her body wanted to do was make it back to the cabin and crumple into bed. But trepidation stayed her.

'Are you going to tell me what that was all about?' she asked at last, as she skied slowly away.

He remained silent.

'I only came on this trip with you because you asked me to. You promised me honesty and you asked for my help,' she reminded him desperately. 'Well, I'm here, fulfilling my promise. Now you need to fulfil yours.'

'Fulfilling your promise like the fact that for five years you kept our baby a secret from me? You've had a chance to mourn what we lost. But you denied me that chance.'

The words hit her with such force she struggled to breathe. He couldn't *really* be throwing that at her now, could he?

'I'm sorry.' He shook his head, devastated. 'I shouldn't have said that.'

'This isn't about the—the baby,' she managed to stutter out. 'This is about *you*.'

'What do you want from me, Thea?' His voice was low, deep, uncompromising. Yet his eyes were ringed with red, glistening.

It took her by surprise. He was a soldier—he saw war, saw lots of things. That he should be so affected by the loss of their baby caught her off guard.

'I don't know.' Thea closed her eyes to hold back her own tears.

He dipped his head. Saying nothing. Busying himself with the snowboard.

Then, in silent unison they skied back down to their cabin.

'You're leaving, aren't you?' Thea asked as they headed inside.

'I have to,' he told her. 'I'm sorry.'

'You can't protect everyone. Even though you might want to,' she whispered as he turned to face her. 'Just don't go getting yourself killed out there.'

'I don't intend to,' he replied gruffly, tilting her head up and kissing her salty tears. 'But I *do* intend to come back for you.'

Her throat felt closed. 'Then you know where to find me.'

But deep down she knew he never would. What Ben needed to do was the one thing he could never do. To open up. To talk about his emotions. But he was Army—through and through. Bottling everything up and hoping he never got shaken.

They stayed in each other's arms for only minutes, but it felt like hours, and she clung to him for as long as she could. When he tore himself away to pack up his belongings and leave the cabin she knew she couldn't watch him leave. Their final embrace would be the memory she held on to—not the sight of him walking out through the door.

Quickly, she stumbled back and into her room. She didn't hear Ben leave, but she felt it when the cabin was suddenly empty. Deep down she knew she would never see Ben Abrams again.

CHAPTER THIRTEEN

BEN EYED THE solid wooden door and, squaring up to it, offered three deep, uniform raps with his knuckles.

'Enter.'

The rich, commanding voice threatened to send him walking away. Instead Ben placed his hand firmly on the door and stepped determinedly inside.

'Hello, Dad.'

Ben knew it would wind the old man up—him marching into his barracks office, in uniform but without an appointment, and not addressing him as Colonel. It wasn't intentional but it was too bad. This wasn't about his dad. This was about *him*. And about Thea.

This was the next crucial step in his plan to win her back. Not that it was much of a plan. Despite being in the military, he'd spent much of his career winging it, making up his own medical procedures as he went along in the desperate need to save a life. The only difference this time was that by winning her back the life he would be saving was his own.

He stared across the desk, prepared to see the inevitable disappointment. However, the man behind the desk looked surprisingly drawn, unusually thin beneath the dark tan from the Afghan sun. He peered over his glasses, and Ben registered a flicker of shock as he made himself stride in confidently.

'I heard you weren't in Afghanistan.' Ben stood in front of the desk. The etiquette drilled into him from childhood

even now precluded him from sitting down until invited.
'I didn't believe it.'

'I came back a while ago.' His father gave an imperceptible gesture and Ben pulled out a chair and sat down
accordingly.

'You weren't planning on being redeployed the last time
I spoke to you,' Ben challenged.

He had crossed paths with his father at their last camp,
a couple of weeks before Ben had been caught in the IED
blasts. Yet Thea said she'd seen his father at the hospital
soon after Ben had been transported back.

'Things…changed.'

*Could his father really have given up his command for
him?* No, he was being fanciful, caught up as he was in
his drive for information. There had to be a more logical
explanation.

'I understand you passed your Medical Board Assessment today, clearing you for active duty? Congratulations.'

'Thank you.' Ben inclined his head.

He'd been in there less than an hour ago, but why should
he be surprised that his father already knew the results?
The Board probably had the Colonel on speed dial.

'However, I won't be returning to active duty. Tomorrow
I'm going to tender my resignation from the British Army,'
he announced quickly, without fanfare. 'I'll be handing my
official letter to my Commanding Officer.'

'I see.'

The Colonel looked grim, and Ben felt a rush of irritation.

'I'm only coming to forewarn you now as a courtesy,
Dad.' He intended to emphasise that it had nothing to do
with his father's position as Battalion IC.

'May I ask what has precipitated this decision?' his father asked stiffly.

'This isn't the life for me any more,' Ben answered simply, surprising even himself with his confidence in his de-

cision. 'I've enjoyed it for twelve years, but it's time for me to move on to new things. I'm not running away.'

He wanted to get that in before his father leaped to his own assumptions. He knew it was true. He was running *towards* something. Towards a new life, a new future, and the only woman he'd ever loved. He just had to convince her that he'd changed enough for her to love him too. Not that his father would ever understand any of that.

'I have *never* known you to run away, Benjamin. Not in the twelve years you've served your country and not as a boy.'

Ben certainly hadn't been prepared for his father's apparent acceptance. He sat, shocked, as his father continued. Awkwardly, but with the resolute glint in his eyes that Ben recognised so well.

'I know you better than you realise, Benjamin. So I understand why you waited to pass your Medical Board before tendering your resignation. You wanted to see your recovery through and you were determined to pass. Because now you can be satisfied that the decision to leave is all yours—no one else's.'

'Right...' Ben frowned. 'Thank you.'

Of all things, his father's understanding, his acceptance, was the last thing he'd expected. He stood up to leave, almost forgetting why he'd wanted to come.

Abruptly he stopped. Turned. 'Did you visit me in the hospital?'

His father hesitated. 'Yes,' he acknowledged after a moment. 'I suppose your young lady told you?'

So Thea *had* seen him. Ben was shocked.

'She's Daniel Fletcher's sister, I understand?'

'Yes,' Ben ground out.

He didn't want to discuss Thea with his father. Didn't want any shadow cast over her. Not by his father—not by anyone.

'She has nothing to do with my decision to leave the

Army.' It wasn't strictly true, but he wasn't leaving *for* Thea. He was leaving for the life he wanted away from the Army, which happened to include Thea.

'Sir James tells me she's a very accomplished young trauma surgeon,' his father continued levelly.

'She is.' Ben felt a rush of pride, momentarily loosening his tongue and making him forget who he was talking to. 'She's one of the most gifted trauma doctors I've known.'

She was also caring, compassionate and strong. *So* strong. And he might have thrown all that away just because he had thought closing himself off emotionally was the *only* way to be strong. She'd shown him how wrong he was. She was the reason he was now able, for the first time in his life, to ask his father questions he would never before have been able to. She had made him realise that this was where he'd learned to suppress his emotions— from his father. But he still didn't understand *why* his father had shut them out.

'Was I the reason you returned from Afghanistan? Gave up your post?'

'Benjamin, I don't think this is the right time for this conversation...'

'*Was* I?' Ben pushed, refusing to back down.

'I... I thought I'd lost you, son.' The Colonel jutted his chin out defiantly but suddenly, if only for an instant, he stopped looking like the driven, emotionless, inflexible Army Colonel Ben knew, and Ben caught a fleeting glimpse of a shaken, frightened, uncertain father.

And then it was gone.

But still, it had caught Ben off guard and unsettled him.

'Where has all this compassion, this emotion been for the last twenty years?' he bit out in frustration. 'Where was all the grief when my mother died?'

He expected his father to shout, to reprimand him for his insolence. Instead the old man offered him a sad smile.

'I was trying to do what was best for you. For us.'

'By getting rid of all traces of her?' Ben shook his head. 'By never discussing her?'

Thea was right—it *wasn't* healthy for anyone to bottle things up. His relationship with his father was a mess. He had no idea if it could ever be repaired—or if his father would ever *want* to repair it. But Ben *did* know that he was going to do everything in his power to salvage his relationship with Thea. She was good for him. She'd helped him heal when he'd never known he was broken. He was never going to find it easy to express how he was feeling, but he now knew he had to try—for himself as much as for Thea. She made him want to be a better person.

'How did you think pretending she'd never existed would help?' Ben urged.

For a moment he thought his father was going to shut down, he could see the old man struggling, but—incredibly—the Colonel met his glower.

'I thought keeping the past behind us would help you to move on. I thought it would help me too.'

To Ben's horror, his father faltered. He had never seen the old man struggle to control his emotions—*any* emotions—before.

'I was wrong. I'm…sorry.'

So Thea had been right along. He needed to tell her that. Needed to tell her how he felt. Everything. Before it was too late.

If it wasn't already.

'I have to go. There's someone I need to talk to.' Ben stalked to the door, hauling it open and striding outside just as his father's parting words reached his ears.

'Perhaps one day you'll allow us to start to rebuild our relationship?'

Ben turned back, the closing door still giving him a visible line to his father.

'One day.' He nodded. 'I'd like that.'

CHAPTER FOURTEEN

THEA SANK DOWN onto the bench to change out of her flight gear. Exhaustion was a daily occurrence these days. She'd told her colleagues nothing more than that Ben had returned to active duty, but as though they'd sensed the depths of her sorrow they had sent as many call-outs as they could her way in order to keep her busy.

She was grateful for the work. It kept her distracted, draining her physically and mentally, so that when she went home to her empty cottage she barely had the energy to sleep, let alone mope or cry.

Deep down she knew Ben was never coming back. As much as he loved her—and she now knew he did—she couldn't compete with the ghosts of the men he had lost, the ghost of Daniel. But it wasn't just the ghosts. It was more about the fact that Ben could never open up to her about it, that he was so emotionally closed off to her even after everything they'd shared. It meant that there could be no future for the two of them.

Stepping out of the shower, she started drying herself. It was an effort to get dressed. If she could have stayed here, slept in the rec room and waited for her next shift, she probably would have done.

She stepped out of the locker room and straight into a solid, well-built body.

'Ben?'

She felt her chest start to bubble and expand as hopeful anticipation jangled wildly. She ruthlessly stamped it down. She'd been here before with Ben. Twice. She couldn't put herself through it a third time. She had to be absolutely certain.

'What are you doing here?' She was proud of how even she'd managed to keep her voice.

His response, however, wasn't as measured.

'Looking for you.'

Her traitorous heart gave a leap of joy before she muffled it into submission.

'I was also signing some paperwork with Sir James.'

'What paperwork?' she asked suspiciously.

'My release forms. From the time I spent here on a consultancy basis.'

Of course he was. He'd need to be cleared in order to go back out on tours of duty. She was an idiot. Thank God she hadn't given in to the urge to race to him.

'When do you ship out?'

He fixed her with a look.

'I don't.'

Thea felt her legs start to weaken but she held her ground. She was relieved. Knowing he was back out there was her worst fear. Still, she felt sympathy for him.

'I'm sorry,' she said sincerely.

Ben frowned. 'What for?'

'The Medical Board? You weren't cleared for active duty?'

His slow, wide smile made her heart falter. It was genuine, but gentle.

'I *was* cleared for active duty. My recovery is better than textbook.'

'You've been incredible.' She'd seen it for herself but it was still impressive. And so typically Ben to make such a startling recovery. She bunched her shoulders. 'But you're not shipping out?'

'I quit,' he said simply, his eyes never leaving her face.

'You...*quit*? The Army? For good?' She was having a hard time getting her head around it.

'For good,' he confirmed patiently.

It was the news she had been longing for—the news she'd never expected to hear. 'What changed your mind?'

'You did,' he answered honestly.

She shook her head. She needed more than that.

'Shall we talk in private?' Ben asked, indicating the main office.

With a nod of acquiescence Thea managed to make her legs move towards the quiet room. Stepping inside, she sat down on a chair and looked at him expectantly.

'What I have to tell you...' Ben sat in front of her, taking her hands in his as he leaned in. 'Well, it isn't going to be easy to hear.'

'Because it's about Daniel?' she acknowledged.

'Yes.'

'I don't think you have a choice, Ben.' She tried to quell the anxious jangles. 'I think you *need* to tell me—whatever it is. I think everything inside you is all hopelessly bound together, and until you actually say the words you've no chance of ever untying it in *here*.' She tapped the side of his head, as if to illustrate her point.

He nodded, but stayed silent, his hands still holding hers.

Thea watched their two sets of hands, together but not quite entwined, unable to draw her gaze away. Eventually the silence weighed too heavily.

'You *have* to tell me, Ben. Whatever it is, I can handle it—as long as you're the one who is telling me.'

'Are you really sure you want to do this, Thea?'

She swallowed hard. *No turning back now.*

'I'm sure.'

Ben nodded, taking a moment as if to compose himself, then starting.

'You once asked me why I *really* married you. I told you that part of it was a promise I made to Daniel.'

Thea nodded.

'You never quite understood—never could see the significance—and I don't blame you. But the truth is I made that promise to him the day he died.'

Thea felt as though wheels were spinning in her head.

'The day he died?' she repeated slowly.

'I'm sorry, Thea. I should have explained it to you a long time ago. When he made me make that promise Dan was dying.'

It sounded as though Ben was trying to talk with a tongue too thick for his mouth. As if it was an effort for his mouth to form the words.

'Pardon?' Thea swallowed hard. A deathbed promise? Had she *really* been prepared to hear this?

'We'd been heading to the front line. There had been a battalion manoeuvre and there were thousands of soldiers out there. Hundreds wounded. They couldn't get the injured back through the lines to our field hospital fast enough. A few two-man medical teams chose to advance, to try to help as many as we could in the field—stabilise them until they could be moved back.'

'You and Daniel were one of those teams?' Her heart was practically battering down her chest wall.

'Yes. We were ahead of the other teams. There was a small enemy section closing in on one flank that no one had seen. We got pinned down and Dan took a bullet. He couldn't move. I was trying to drag him behind some rocks for cover when we fell into a foxhole in the dirt. We stayed there whilst I tried to stem the bleeding, but…he was badly hit.'

'He was dying?' Thea whispered, lifting her head to look at Ben.

'I'm sorry.' His eyes pinned her in place. Sincere and full of apology. 'You asked for the truth.'

So help her, she had.

'I was concentrating on stemming the wound. Trying to see if there was any way I could possibly get us out of there. But they were all around us. Searching for us. We could hear them passing less than a foot away. It was all Dan could do not to make a noise.'

No, Thea realised, *because even if he'd known he was dying he would never have wanted to risk his best friend's life.*

'When he realised he was dying he made me promise to take care of you. I think, deep down, he knew I hadn't got over you. Just as I told you he knew that I'd used our "buddy code" as an excuse to back away.'

'Yet he still trusted you enough to ask you to take care of me...as he died?' she said, feeling rattled.

So this was why Ben had never been able to talk about it. The more he revealed, the more she understood why he found it so hard to talk about himself. She almost laughed at the absurdity of it.

Instead a tear escaped and slid down her cheek.

'Thank you for telling me. It was...*is*...important to me.'

'It doesn't bring him back, though,' Ben stated sadly.

'No, it doesn't.'

Aside from the promise, none of these facts about Dan's death were a great revelation to her. But she could see the strides forward Ben had made in order to finally tell her all that. To finally begin to face up to the emotional toll it had taken on him.

'Because he'd trusted me that much I was determined to set aside my own fears and support you whenever you needed me. Instead we slept together. I felt as though I'd failed even in *that*. I couldn't talk to you about it—I couldn't talk to anyone. So I did what I believed you wanted and I left. I let you down...over and over again. Just as I'd feared I would.'

'I wanted to help you, when you were first injured, but you wouldn't let me.'

'How could I? I'd let you down and I'd shut you out— time and again. How could I accept your help and be so indebted to you when I couldn't even tell you how I felt?

It's taken time, and an incredible amount of patience on your part, but you've begun to change all that.'

'Really?'

She clearly desperately wanted to believe him, but he couldn't blame her for holding back. It was almost ironic. She had helped him to open up about his emotions and his actions had caused her to become more guarded.

'Yes,' he said earnestly. 'You *have*. And not only that you've taught me how to love, unconditionally, for the first time since my mother died.'

'I have?'

Ben dipped his head in confirmation.

'My father and I have had a...complicated relationship. Growing up, I learned that people weren't capable of loving each other without hurting each other, or letting them down. So I overthought everything, always calculating the risk. But then you came along and taught me that love isn't about risk calculations or logic. It's about taking a leap of faith and trusting my heart. And I trust my heart when I'm with you.'

It took every last bit of Thea's self-control not to let him gather her into the strong arms which she remembered too well. She wanted so much to believe Ben, but doubts still lurked.

'I thought you were getting there on the ski trip, and then...' She tailed off helplessly.

'I *was* getting there,' he assured her. 'But things were so close to surface back then, I suppose. Then you told me about the baby and I think it just tipped things again.'

'I'm sorry. I shouldn't have said anything.'

'Of course you should have. I needed to know as much as you needed to tell me. I just wasn't prepared. I hadn't quite processed it. I was still reeling. Every time I turned around it seemed that my inability to open up to you had just caused more and more ripple effects, each one more devastating than the last. You'd lost a baby, *our* baby, and

I'd left you to deal with it all on your own. The one person I was meant to look after and protect, and instead I'd made things worse for you.'

'So when you saw that skier the next day you just re-acted?'

'I thought—stupidly—that it was one thing I could control. One thing I could do right and help someone.'

'So what's changed?' It was difficult to believe it had been that easy.

'I lost you,' he answered simply. 'You'd been there for me and I let the best thing in my life slip away from me. I knew I had to win you back, and the only way to do that was to deal with all the issues I've spent years—some *twenty* years—bottling up. And that's because of you. You have helped me to heal.'

'But your Medical Board…?'

'I realised I didn't want to go back on active duty a long time ago. I wanted a different life. A life with you in it. The only reason I took that assessment was so that I could turn it down. Simply to prove to you that making a life with you was my first choice. Not a fallback. The minute I lost you, out on that mountain, I knew I'd messed up. You are the only thing that matters, and I'm willing to do whatever it takes to win you back.'

'So you passed the Board so that you could leave the Army?'

'Yes,' Ben said simply. 'And, for what it's worth, the assessment was intensive, rigorous, and full of questions. Yet nothing fazed me. I didn't have flashbacks, or moments of anxiety or anger, and I didn't shut down. I just told the Board what they wanted to know. I recounted what had happened factually, but not with any need for clinical de-tachment. And that's all down to you. Getting me to talk, to open up, to acknowledge how I was feeling. You've helped me to heal what I didn't even know before was broken.'

Thea couldn't help but begin to believe him as she con-

sidered the man in the chair opposite her. Sitting back com-
fortably, his hands resting together, his eyes meeting hers
easily, he was a far cry from the man of several months
ago who had sat ramrod-straight, his fists clenching and
unclenching on his knees, refusing to meet her eye but staring fixedly out of the window as each word was wrenched
from him.

'So you've really left?'

'I've really left,' he confirmed. 'I've given the Army
twelve years of my life. I've served with honour and I've
loved almost every minute. But now it's time for a new
chapter in my life. A chapter that includes you and hope-
fully our children.'

'I'd like that too…' Thea bit her lip.

He saw she still wasn't sure about him, and the realisation felt like a punch in the guts. He focused on the hope
flickering in her eyes.

'But you still don't believe me?'

He felt as if it was all sliding away, and he was frantically grasping at the remnants of what might have been.

'I believe that you're sincere, and that you've turned a
corner. But, Ben, you don't have to be in a war zone with
the Army to find ways of risking your life. You ran towards
a burning car when you were with the Air Ambulance. You
crossed an avalanche-struck slope on a *ski holiday.*'

Ben stared at her incredulously. 'To save *lives.* You and
I both know that if I hadn't that baby, and Tomas, would
have been dead by the time anyone else got there. If someone's life is in danger I have to help—that's just who I am.'

'I know that,' Thea assured him. 'And I would never
expect you to walk away from someone in need. But the
way you do it—running blindly in, with no regard for your
own safety—that scares me.'

'Then what do you propose?' He held his hands out desperately. He couldn't lose her. Not now.

'A trial period,' she said at last. 'For our relationship and for the Air Ambulance.'

'What does that mean?' Ben asked carefully.

'At work you're always going to be the one who risks his life for others—look at your Distinguished Service Order, look at the men you pulled to safety after that bomb blast even when you only had one arm. I'm not trying to change that. But just take a moment—one minute, thirty seconds, fifteen seconds—that's all I ask. To talk to me, or anyone, so that I know you've assessed the danger. So that I know you're taking calculated risks, not reckless ones. So that I don't feel so helpless.'

'I can do that,' Ben agreed slowly.

He understood exactly where she was coming from, and he respected her strength of character. He was impetuous, she was right about that, and he needed someone who cared enough about him to pull him up over it. He knew Thea was that person.

'And as for our relationship...'

This was the bit he really wanted to know. He had to convince Thea that she was all that mattered to him. Without her, his life was empty.

'We spend time together,' she said simply. 'We get to know each other. Sometimes we do boring, mundane things, like going to the cinema, instead of you wanting me try base jumping or something equally adrenalin-fuelled.'

He nodded. He'd always used that kind of stuff as a distraction—especially around anniversaries—to avoid having to think about how he felt. But with Thea he didn't feel he needed those safety nets any more.

'Learning about each other...talking,' he agreed with a grin. 'I can do that.'

'It doesn't mean we can't have fun together.' She smiled.

'Does this trial period include separate bedrooms?' he asked, suddenly straight-faced. 'Because if it does, I can tell you that's a deal-breaker.'

'It does *not* include separate rooms.' She laughed softly.

'OK, then.' His gaze never left hers as he became serious again. 'I'll give you as long as you need. Until you know that you have nothing left to fear. I intend to put you—our family—first from now on.'

'Then I think you'd better sign some new paperwork,' she choked out, tears spilling over as Ben crossed the divide between them in one smooth movement and lifted her up from her chair into his arms, his mouth coming down to claim hers.

It was a kiss full of hope, full of promise, and one day soon he hoped it would turn into one free of any lingering reservations.

'And when you finally trust me completely I promise you I'm going to carry you over that damned threshold, Mrs Abrams.' His lips rumbled against hers as they finally came up for air.

'I hope you can fulfil that promise, because I'd like that, Mr Abrams,' Thea murmured. 'I'd like that very much.'

EPILOGUE

Five years later

'HAPPY TENTH ANNIVERSARY, Mrs Abrams.' Ben kissed her gently awake as the first rays of dawn poured through a gap in the curtains.

'Happy tenth anniversary,' she mumbled sleepily, wrapping her arms around his neck and getting ready to pull him back into bed for a proper good morning celebration.

But Ben quickly detached her grip with a rumble of amusement.

'Sorry, my love, but no time. You'd better brace yourself.'

'Brace myself...?'

'Happy Mummy's day to you, Happy Mummy's day to you...'

Their three-year-old burst excitedly into the room with a delightfully out of tune, improvised rendition of 'Happy Birthday'. She stopped, glancing at him for guidance, and Ben was only too happy to jump into the fray and sing along with his daughter.

Then, waving a handmade card with a colourful, splodgy footprint on the front, she leapt onto the bed, and Ben felt a burst of pride as he watched his little girl snuggle up to her mummy, almost shoving the card up Thea's nose in her eagerness.

'I made it for you, Mummy. It's my footprint—see?'

She waggled her foot in the air, as if fearing her mother wouldn't recognise it otherwise, and Ben was amused to see Thea actually checking the foot. Mercifully, it was clean—which was more than could be said for the bathroom floor right now.

As Thea shifted up the bed to wrap her daughter in her arms Ben lurched forward to help her.

She batted him away good-naturedly. 'I'm pregnant. I'm not ill.'

'I know that, but you're over a week overdue and you look ready to pop,' he chastised her as a fresh surge of love crashed over him.

'Which is why they'll be inducing me on Wednesday if he hasn't been born by then. I'd say he's definitely *your* son.' Thea shot him a wicked grin. 'He won't arrive until he's good and ready.'

'A brother, a brother... I'm getting a brother,' came a sing-song cry of delight. Then the little girl stopped, a look of concern clouding her perfect features. 'Do you think he'll know that it's my birthday next weekend?'

'I'm pretty sure he will,' Thea reassured her, with a quick glance to Ben.

He nodded in confirmation. He had collected a couple of gifts and some party supplies yesterday, knowing that it would reassure Thea. She was adamant that this would be the first party their three-year-old daughter would remember, so they were going to throw one this year.

With all the attention she knew was bound to be lavished on their new son by well-meaning friends, Thea was determined not to let their daughter feel even a little bit left out.

She was an incredible mother. An incredible woman. After the bad start their marriage had suffered, those first five years, Ben had been determined to ensure these last five years had been the best years of her life. They had certainly been the best of his.

They worked alongside each other occasionally, but staggered their shift patterns so that one of them was almost always home with their incredible little girl. He couldn't be happier. Except, perhaps, when their new son joined them properly and they would be a foursome.

'Come on, munchkin.' Ben leaned over the bed and swung his daughter up. An excited shriek came from the little girl. 'I promised you a morning in the park whilst your mummy sleeps. She might have a busy day ahead of her soon.'

'Um, Ben—'

The catch in her voice made him spin around quickly.

'I think that day is now. I've been having light contractions all night, and my waters have just broken.'

'We're going in?' Ben confirmed.

Last time Thea had taken a bath and baked her favourite carrot cake before finally letting him drive her to the hospital.

Thea pushed herself out of bed and took her daughter for a last cuddle. 'Phone the Colonel first.'

'Colonel Grandpa! Colonel Grandpa!' The little girl jiggled, delighted at the fulfilment of a long-standing promise of a day or two exclusively with her grandfather.

Ben grabbed her and tickled her, before she could kick Thea to bits in her excitement.

Funny how the term *Colonel* was now used affectionately to refer to his father. Ben had never expected to have a good relationship with him, but things had changed a lot over the last five years. And the old man positively doted on his granddaughter.

'I'll be back in a few minutes,' Ben said, placing the wriggling three-year-old on the floor, She raced out through the door to find Ben's phone. He cast Thea a glance. 'And then we'll get ready to welcome our son into the world.'

'Our new bundle of joy.' Thea smiled softly.

'To go with our beautiful daughter.' Ben beamed proudly. 'Have I told you yet today how much I love you, Mrs Abrams?'

'No,' Thea teased. 'So tell me now.'

* * * * *

MILLS & BOON®
Hardback – June 2016

ROMANCE

MILLS & BOON®
Large Print – June 2016

ROMANCE

Leonetti's Housekeeper Bride	Lynne Graham
The Surprise De Angelis Baby	Cathy Williams
Castelli's Virgin Widow	Caitlin Crews
The Consequence He Must Claim	Dani Collins
Helios Crowns His Mistress	Michelle Smart
Illicit Night with the Greek	Susanna Carr
The Sheikh's Pregnant Prisoner	Tara Pammi
Saved by the CEO	Barbara Wallace
Pregnant with a Royal Baby!	Susan Meier
A Deal to Mend Their Marriage	Michelle Douglas
Swept into the Rich Man's World	Katrina Cudmore

HISTORICAL

Marriage Made in Rebellion	Sophia James
A Too Convenient Marriage	Georgie Lee
Redemption of the Rake	Elizabeth Beacon
Saving Marina	Lauri Robinson
The Notorious Countess	Liz Tyner

MEDICAL

Playboy Doc's Mistletoe Kiss	Tina Beckett
Her Doctor's Christmas Proposal	Louisa George
From Christmas to Forever?	Marion Lennox
A Mummy to Make Christmas	Susanne Hampton
Miracle Under the Mistletoe	Jennifer Taylor
His Christmas Bride-to-Be	Abigail Gordon